Mag...

and other stories

Magician

and other stories

Ivy Bannister

Good luck to
Sean!
from
Ivy

POOLBEG

Published 1996
by Poolbeg Press Ltd
123 Baldoyle Industrial Estate
Dublin 13, Ireland

© Ivy Bannister 1996

The moral right of the author has been asserted.

The Publishers gratefully acknowledge the support of The Arts Council.

A catalogue record for this book is available from the British Library.

ISBN 1 85371 675 8

Cover painting: *Innocence* c. 1830, National Gallery of Art, Washington
Cover design by Poolbeg Group Services Ltd
Set by Poolbeg Group Services Ltd in Goudy 11.5/14.5
Printed by The Guernsey Press Ltd,
Vale, Guernsey, Channel Islands.

About the Author

Ivy Bannister was born in New York City and educated at Smith College, Massachusetts and Trinity College, Dublin. Her stories have been published and anthologised widely, and broadcast by RTE and the BBC. Plays have been performed in Derry and Germany, and on radio. She has received several awards, including the Hennessy Award in 1988 and the Mobil Ireland Playwrighting Award in 1993. The Arts Council granted her a bursary in literature in 1994. Known to lecture occasionally on literature and drama, Ivy writes regularly for *Image* and RTE's *Sunday Miscellany*.

She lives in Dublin with her husband and their two sons. *Magician* is her first collection.

Acknowledgements

These stories have been published and broadcast as follows, sometimes in different forms: Magician in *London Magazine* and on RTE Radio 1; The Family Life of Jimmy McManus in *London Magazine*; My Mother's Daughter on RTE Radio 1 and in *Prize Winning Radio Stories*; Seduced in *The Irish Times*, *Virgins and Hyacinths* and *U*; Words on RTE Radio 1 and in *Woman's Way*; Happy Delivery in *Iron* and on BBC Radio 4; Dublin is Full of Married Men in *U* and on BBC Radio 4; Underwear on BBC Radio 4; The Chiropodist in *Panurge*, *Move Over Waxblinder!*, on BBC Radio 4, and as a play on RTE Radio 1; Lift Me Up and Pour Me Out in the *Cork Examiner*, *21 All Told* and as a play on RTE Radio 1; The Naughty Bits in the *Irish Press* (for which it received a Hennessy Award) and *The Salmon*.

For

Hortense and Richard

Table of Contents

Magician

He keeps the lady rabbits in a spacious hutch at the end of the garden, near the airy cage where the lovebirds flirt and coo. Their drinking water sparkles out from a fountain, blue as his own eyes, and there's enough greenery for a jungle. They are well looked after, Zeno's rabbits and birds, for when it comes to the tools of his trade, Zeno is more than particular.

But that being said, Zeno's arrangements for Mister Buggs are in a class of their own. Believe it or not, that oversized white buck rabbit is allowed to sleep in our own four-poster bed, burrowing his way deep into the quilt, curling himself right around Zeno's feet. In the morning, I have to pluck his rabbit hairs out from the down, one by one.

To my mind that rabbit is overfed, overpampered and overindulged. But I keep my opinions to myself. I wouldn't cross Zeno, at least not if he had a ghost of a chance of finding me out. For I've learned plenty during

1

all my years with Zeno. I've learned that there's great power in a clear mind and a silent tongue, because – at the end of the day – what is magic, only getting what you want without showing how.

So I brush my hair when Zeno fools with that rabbit, when he paddles his hands in the lush white fur, kneading and rubbing until Mister Buggs positively purrs. I brush my hair with the ivory-backed hairbrush until my arm aches, but I sing a carefree song. And even when Zeno decides that the lady rabbits require servicing, I smile pleasantly, then follow them both out to the hutch; and there, in the moonlight, I ooh and ahh as Mister Buggs does his business. There's a glow and gleam in Zeno's eyes as Mister Buggs spreads it around. He is so proud of that rabbit, my Zeno. Yes, he is puffed with pride that his ageing protégé can still frolic with a full hutch. Men!

Still, Zeno is a fine man himself, the kind you'd see once, then never forget. His black curls and Latin skin make the blue of his eyes the more remarkable. The sight of his muscular body poured into that dress-suit under the hot stage lights still makes me catch my breath. And his hands! His dancing hands! Even though I know those hands better than anyone, I could watch them forever, drawing silk out of silk, as the audience gasps with amazement. Legerdemain, levitation, illusion: there is nothing too impossible for Zeno.

He has an extraordinary power over women. Young and old, they follow him around the circuit, watching his performances, roaring and applauding, night after night.

But the men like him too. They see in Zeno the big man that they long to become. Zeno the Magnificent – that's what he's known as – Zeno the Magnificent.

He had an extraordinary power over me. In my youth, I was mesmerised. I used to let him saw me in two, and not think twice about it. When I remember the clothes that I wore for him! The sequinned bodice that made my breasts look like luscious melons, the saucy fish-net tights, the red sateen shoes with their stiletto heels that sparked off the floor. To tell the truth, I rather liked wearing those clothes. Then. But I wouldn't let him away with such nonsense anymore. No way would I dress up like a bimbo now, not just to show off his mystique. No, I have grown too much in stature.

But I was there for him in the beginning, heart and soul. I believed in him when nobody else did. I played my part in making him the man that he is. And no way am I going to let him go, not without letting loose a few thunderbolts of my own.

I wonder, did that woman seduce him through his stomach? Did she tempt him out of his trousers by the calculated preparation of irresistible morsels: tartlets and tidbits? Did her spicy canapés make him hunger for something more substantial? I used to cook for him like that myself, before I got sense. Yes, Zeno and I would lick and nibble together, beginning with one another's fingers, before bringing the shutters down on time to leave no parts untouched.

Our union was fruitful. Half a dozen lively babes kicked their way into our world. Proof positive of our root togetherness! And what fine young creatures they've grown into: bright and wilful, ready to grab life by the throat and give it a shaking.

The fact is, that as a family we've been showered with blessings. For our health and comfort, Zeno has plucked a rainbow of coins out of the air. We live in a palace of a house, the largest of a trio that harbours the successful: a cabinet minister; a lady who writes naughty books; and us. Stretching in front of our home, there's a lawn and a river. Behind it, there's a forest. And inside? There are eight bedrooms with pink-and-white striped wallpaper. In our en suite bathrooms, the basins are porcelain and the taps are gold. This is truly a house that any woman would desire. That's the sting of it. This seductress covets what belongs to me.

It was Mister Buggs who led me by the nose to the first letter. There I was relaxing, feet up, painting my nails calypso pink, when I heard that damned rabbit thumping his hind legs on the floor to gain my attention. "What is it now?" I snarled, not troubling to disguise my tone of voice, since Zeno was out for the day. Mister Buggs simply stared, a knowing look in his malevolent pink eyes. "Bugger off, Mister Buggs," I yawned, but he thumped and thumped again, until there was nothing for it, but to follow his white scut out the door, around to the shady side of the house, where the waste pipe empties from the utility room. And there, amidst the sludge and domestic offal, I found a wisp of paper. A letter. A letter from her, that female-creature, blocked out in her kiddy hand.

"To my Silver-Tongued Zeno," I read, "I love Golden

4

Retriever puppies and raspberry crumble and you." That was the sum of it, the trollop's scrawl, unsigned except for the infinite kisses marked in Xs and Os across the bottom of the page. I tell you, my tears fell onto that letter, smearing her violet ink so that it stained my hand. I could smell her cheap perfume, supermarket scent squirted from an aerosol. I could picture her – slinky lamé dress melting onto the floor as she stepped out of it – thrilled with her own bravado for wearing no underwear. I could even imagine the big Z, tattooed in roses upon her scrawny haunch. All for Zeno, my lover, the father of my children. With my teeth, I tore at her letter, shredding its substance until only the words remained engraved inside my head. Mister Buggs watched me, his whiskery snout twisting into a leer.

I wonder: does Zeno pull her into the bed by her nipple as he used to pull me?

Of course once I knew about the one letter, I couldn't rest easy. I realised that there must be more, and there were: nameless flutterings spilling out from pocket and drawer, rustling under radiators and nestling in books. Relentlessly, I hunted them out, emptying vases and pulling out cushions. From room to room Mister Buggs followed me, the claws on his rabbit's toes scratching upon the wooden floor. There was strut to his scamper, as he flaunted his joy in my humiliation. Yes, I knew what was going on inside his fuzzy rabbit's brain. Mister Buggs believed that he had me somewhere beneath his pudgy paw, where every buck rabbit imagines he can relegate the females in his life.

When I had them all, all her letters, I spread them out, wispy tissues on the solid table where Zeno and the family eat. Pouring over every squiggle and blot, I pieced together my rival's portrait. It was there, all there. The long blonde hair and the games that she played with it; the smell of ripe fruit; the witchery of a woman who smiles with her body; her armoury of feathers and leathers and stimulating creams. I pressed my nose close against the window of her passion, and I shivered. But then, at last, tucked in a tiny corner, I discovered her name. Meggy!

Meggy? What was that, only a hidey-hole of a name. Meggy? A name for a nymph too green to face the substance of Margaret or Marjorie. Yes, for when I thought about that silly name, I realised I would win. For suddenly I understood the artlessness of her damned tricks. After all, hadn't I played a version of every one of them myself, once upon a time when I was only a slip of a thing?

Oh my beloved Zeno, how could you conjure with another woman after magicking my own body? Do you think me still a baby? Don't you know that we've grown up? Don't you realise that I have earned your respect, that I deserve better, that we have become equals?

Mister Buggs thumped his hind legs on the floor and gloated, intoxicated by his imagined success. No doubt he already pictured himself inching his way up our bed, climbing the slippery pole from Zeno's foot-warmer to pride of place on my very pillow itself.

Silly rabbit!

But I pretended to be beaten. I looked down at him and cowered, subservient before the Great God Rabbit that he believed himself to be. I even managed a few tears, shimmering things that tumbled charmingly down my cheeks. They were a trick of my own, I confess, calculated to sweeten my pleasure in revenge. For if in my youth I was inclined to let life unfold whatever way it liked, now I blow up bridges. Yes, I have come of age. I am forty-two years old and in my prime. I unashamedly relish every single thing that I do.

When at last I set about it, I proceeded in the French manner. You might describe my preparations as sensuous. Thoughtfully, I culled the rosemary: best sprigs only, picked in the garden under his watchful eye. Then, unblemished potatoes, their new skins fine enough to eat. Peppercorns for spice. He actually sat on the draining board grooming his white fur as I scraped the carrots, imagining, I suppose, that I was doing the carrots for him. Which in a way I was.

I performed the disagreeable bit with one of Zeno's own belts, the green one with the buckle shaped like a Z and studded with rhinestones. I tightened it notch by notch around his hairy neck until he twitched no more, until his mouth gaped, his buck teeth protruding in an unseemly fashion. Then with a sharp knife I slit him open, flinging his guts onto a pyre fashioned out of Meggy's letters, and I watched them burn together. The grey smoke floated up into the night sky. No, my Zeno's fingers will paddle no more in the lush fur of others.

After it has been cooked, the meat itself bears a

remarkable similarity to chicken in colour and texture. Layered with vegetables beneath a puff pastry, it presents a most appetising-looking creation indeed. "Sim Sala Bim," I murmured. The ancient incantation hovered in the air, then as I waved my arm like a wand, the pastry rose and a seductive aroma filled the house.

Zeno was charmed at first whiff. He ate greedily, eyes glazing over, as with each pungent mouthful, he slipped deeper and deeper into my power. I heaped his plate a second time.

"Meggy," I whispered cautiously. "Have you ever heard of a woman named Meggy?"

"Who?" he asked, brushing the name away like a fly.

I smiled. I patted his hand. I could see only my own reflection in the brilliant blue of his eyes. The man was mine, all mine, for whatever whimsy I desired.

Zeno. Tonight before we sleep, he will pay me court. He will kiss my feet and rub my back. He is my King, but I am his Queen. And should he ever get out of hand again, which I consider most unlikely, I am sure that I can design another device. For my imagination is as fertile as my body. You might say that I have become something of a magician myself.

The Family Life
of Jimmy McManus

Hello! Jimmy McManus is the name, and my profession is death. I always say it straight out, because I'm proud of what I do. A good undertaker, or mortician as they say in America, is an artist, and a better artist than some who go by the name these days. I've no time for these modernistic chancers who paint trees that are only a mess of colours, and people that look like blobs. My own work is in the classical tradition. The challenge is to make my subject look better in the coffin than he or she did in real life; and up until now, I've been pretty good at it.

Sometimes I work from a photograph, but in this case, it's not necessary. This time I know exactly what I'm aiming for, and I'd like to get it right. There's a superior casket waiting in the anteroom. It's solid oak with brass fittings and a hinged lid. Inside, everything's perfect.

Little pillows for her head and arms, the usual plastic lining – weatherproofing, if you like. In addition, there's twenty-one yards of fine white silk, laced back and forth in airy folds, a bed as soft and smooth as you could imagine.

White silk, as if she were a bride. Yes. This one is a special case. This beautiful creature who lies naked before me is Alice. She used to be my wife, a happy state that regrettably came to an end a year or so before her death. As I wash her slight, willowy body for the last time, I think affectionately of Horace. A gentleman and a scholar, Horace. Large as an overstuffed teddy bear, and generous to a fault. Indeed, I am grateful that Horace regards me highly enough to have engaged my services for the second time. For Alice will be the second wife of Horace's whom I've had the privilege of burying.

It's an interesting story, one that begins at the waste grounds in Booterstown, a suburb of Dublin, on the day that I first met Alice, twenty-three years ago. The attraction was a travelling funfair that had lured us both. I noticed Alice at once; her delicate form, dressed all in white, weaved in and out of the crowd like an angel. I could not tear my eyes away, and, indeed, I followed her as closely as I dared. When she joined the queue for the Big Wheel, I slipped in behind her, close enough so that the white gossamer of her skirt brushed against my trouser leg, and I shivered with pleasure. By chance, the boy operating the carriages assumed that we were together, so I jumped in beside her, the boy fastening the bar over our middles quick as a wink.

In a moment, we were swept off into the sky, the two of us alone in our metal cage. To my surprise, my companion seemed unoffended by my intrusion. Instead, she smiled vaguely, as we whirled round and round in silence. Suddenly, the Big Wheel jolted to a standstill, leaving us stranded at the top. What more could a young man wish for than to be alone with such a creature, suspended in the blue, with an excellent vista of Dublin Bay stretched out before us? I found my tongue and began to talk, pointing out the sights. She seemed to absorb my every word, her eyes wandering towards each landmark as I observed it.

When I paused for breath, she fluttered her lashes. "My name is Alice," she said. She stretched down to her dangling feet and cautiously removed a shoe, which she handed to me.

I considered the shoe with delight. It was tiny, sized only two and a half, as I learned later. It was made of soft leather, lavender in colour, with pale lemon trimmings. The toe curved into a feminine point, and a dainty knob served for heel. The shoe was nearly too pretty to use.

"Mind that for me," she said, reaching down for the other. "And this one too. I don't want to lose them."

The shoes were warm in my hands. In touching them, I imagined that I was touching her body. Her dark eyes were almond-shaped like an Oriental's, and I believe that she was reading my mind.

"I only wear white," she observed. "My entire wardrobe holds nothing but white garments. White blouses and skirts, white dresses, coats and stockings. My undergarments are especially white. Because I wear only white on my body, I can choose whatever colour I like for my shoes."

She tilted her head at me playfully. "I can, and I do."

I felt dizzy with desire. The sea breeze rocked our carriage gently. Her dark eyes seemed to encourage me. With my free hand, I reached out to stroke her cheek. She sighed with pleasure. The skin beneath my fingers was as silky as the petal of a rose.

The wonder is that Alice's skin hasn't changed, not perceptibly. As Alice lies here on my worktable, her skin remains that of a young girl. It retains its wonderful colour, and also the elasticity that is generally so quick to go after the heart stops. Considering these paradoxes, I pat her toes dry with the utmost care. I ease the white stockings onto her feet. Surprisingly, Horace has failed to include any shoes with the rest of her things. He knows as well as anyone else how Alice felt about shoes. I will telephone and ask him to bring the lavender ones with the lemon trim. She never threw out a pair of shoes, not Alice. She minded them as carefully as children, and only rarely had need of a cobbler.

We were trapped together, Alice and I, in that airy paradise for twenty minutes. It was enough. By the time the machine cranked back into action, the die was cast. I was besotted, and she, perhaps more practically, had recognised in me the strength that she needed for herself. She already knew that I would look after her, defer to her, even worship her. She was not a strong woman physically, and, like a vine, needed someone to cast her tendrils around. With relief she abandoned her job as a clerk in the civil service and moved into my house to make it her own.

I was happy to follow her instructions, as dark carpets were torn up, walls painted white, and yellowing blinds taken down. Our bedroom became a spacious haven with billowing curtains, the only ornaments being Alice's shoes, lined up all the way round the walls. They glittered and shone like jewels. Golden party shoes with four-inch lifts. Open-toed magenta wedgies. Sandals with puffs of black feather over the toes. Lord, how I loved all those little shoes. I cared for them as passionately as Alice did herself. I wish that those shoes were still in the house where we lived together. Perhaps I should ask Horace for the entire collection. What other man could have the same associations with those shoes that I have?

Eighteen months after our marriage, Alice's and my happiness was crowned by the birth of a baby. Together we chose the name Finbar, a name that we understood to mean "white-haired." Finbar Joseph McManus. I was told later that the boy was born with his eyes open. Certainly his eyes were a prominent feature, watchful from the beginning, almond-shaped and dark like his mother's.

"The nurse says that he's a remarkable child," Alice told me.

"Why?"

"Because most babies are born with blue eyes."

I was delighted because, like any father, I believed that my baby was special from the beginning. I was a doting daddy. I changed nappies long before it was fashionable for a father to sully his hands. I did my stint with bottles, and I thought nothing of walking Finbar up and down the corridor for long hours when he was colicky.

Alice adored the boy as much as I did. She would sit him up on her knee with a ball of wool. He loved the soft filaments and tore at them for hours. When he tired of the wool, he would grab Alice's hair and give himself over to the pleasure of letting its fine blond strands slip back and forth through his fingers. When I looked at them, my white-haired baby in Alice's arms, I could hardly believe my own good fortune.

The child progressed swiftly. He was crawling at seven months and walking at ten. At a year, we bought him a climbing frame. In no time at all, he was flying from bar to bar like a monkey. His legs were wiry with muscles, a real little boy's legs. And the young rascal was bright as well as agile. He taught himself to read by picking out the words on cereal packets. In a moment of affectionate weakness, I promised him whatever books or comics he wanted. The pup took me at my word, and hundreds of copies of the *Dandy* and the *Beano* passed through his eager hands.

Finbar never reads now, not as far as I know.

Like any child, Finbar took a healthy interest in what his Daddy did. I encouraged it. When Finbar was seven, I brought him into this very room, to show him exactly what I did. Why shouldn't he be proud of his Daddy, like any youngster?

I'd sit Finbar up close to this same worktable, his little

legs dangling, because they weren't yet long enough to reach the floor. He'd study the remains closely, always pleased if it were a man, because that meant a lathering and a shaving. He'd watch as I plumped out the cheeks with cotton wool, and slipped small lozenges under the eyelids to restore their shape. He would even thread the needle for me to stitch the lower lip up through the nose, thus stopping the jaw from gaping at an inappropriate moment. And when I was working on the lips, coaxing them into a beatific smile, Finbar always let me know when I hadn't got it right.

He had a very helpful nature then.

I was proud of the way that Finbar behaved while I worked. He sat patiently, motionless, keen not to miss a thing. Most children wouldn't be half so good.

I had definite ideas about the rearing of children, ideas which I still hold by. It all boils down to five simple precepts:

1. Identify what they're interested in.
2. Give them plenty of it.
3. Show them the world.
4. Censor nothing.
5. Encourage them to express themselves.

"Say what you are thinking, straight out," I said to Finbar. "Don't try to disguise it." A father's responsibility is to open doors. I hope that Finbar will do the same for his own children, should he ever have any, however improbable that seems now.

I don't doubt that Alice supported my views on the rearing of Finbar. I often told her what I thought. She listened, occasionally smiling her pretty smile or nodding her head. Alice was never one for debate. If her views were different, she kept them to herself. At any rate, she didn't interfere with our outings, no more than I interrupted her own routines with the boy.

They adored one another. The house rocked with their secret laughter. Finbar enjoyed dressing up, and what child could have resisted the lure of Alice's shoes? Often, he could be found admiring himself in the mirror, a white garment draped over his lithe form, one stunning pair of shoes or another, peeping out from underneath. They had a way with each other then, Alice and Finbar. They had that special deep intimacy that few mothers and sons enjoy.

Finbar refuses to talk about Alice now. When I ask him how he feels, he scuttles out of the room.

Our leisure time was invariably passed by the seaside. When the business was thriving and money was plentiful, we'd take our summer holiday in Dingle or in Donegal. How Finbar loved those lonely beaches. Wet from the sea, he'd roll on the sand, coating himself in camouflaging grit until he looked like stone, only his white hair betraying his boyhood. Then he'd sit motionless, except for his darting eyes which followed the soaring seabirds. He'd watch and listen, until he could mimic the cries of gull, tern and sandpiper in a clear penetrating tone. Alice and I were dazzled. We held hands and marvelled at what we had created together. The boy was so beautiful. So unearthly. So talented.

Yes, I have many memories. Wonderful memories that fill my head with the pictures and aromas of a perfect past. I have only to close my eyes. Sometimes I imagine that if I dream hard enough, it will all become real again.

Looking back, it's tempting to imagine that there might have been a turning point where two possibilities presented themselves, but where the incorrect option was chosen. The problem is that I don't really understand Finbar, not the young man that he is now, nor the teenager that he became.

If only we had had another child, Alice and I. God knows, I wanted more children. Had the decision been mine, we would have had a family-sized family. But Finbar's birth had been difficult. It took months for Alice to heal inside. To tell you the truth, we grew out of the habit of physical intimacy.

I never believed that this was permanent. I looked ahead to a time when we would make love again, and engender a whole tribe of little McManuses. I was patient. I invented new ways of being close. I bought a second-hand encyclopaedia, and in the evenings I'd read out loud, volume after volume. I tried to get Alice to read too, but she said that she'd rather listen, which she did, holding my hand, half smiling, staring with her ebony eyes.

Maybe I talked too much.

It's so quiet in our home now. Finbar keeps mostly to himself in the room he has made his own. When he surfaces, I can't squeeze two words out of him. When I speak, he doesn't listen, not like Alice did. His watchful eyes twitch. His elbow floats up towards the ceiling, as if it were drawn by a string. The forearm and hand dangle.

It is not easy being a father.

After young Finbar had mastered his climbing frame, he moved on to the huge oaks at the end of our garden. He learned how to shimmy aloft and leap from branch to branch. In time, those trees became his second home. He could hang upside down, well above the ground, sucking an ice-pop or reading a comic. The onset of winter never stopped him. Indeed, he seemed to prefer the trees when their leaves offered no resistance. I bought him a stout rope, which he'd loop over a branch. He could drop like a stone, using the rope to break his fall only inches from the ground, where he'd land as lightly as a feather. Such wonderful agility.

I encouraged him too when I discovered the spiders, six of them, in jamjars in his room. I purchased an ant farm and a splendid book on insects. He was happy with the ant farm, although later I discovered that he had fed the ants to his spiders. But he turned his nose up at the book.

"A spider isn't an insect," the boy complained. "It's an arachnid. Do you know how many arachnids there are?"

It was not a subject to which I had given much attention.

"Forty thousand of them, Dad," he explained eagerly. "And that's only the ones that have been identified. There may be 80,000 more. Have you ever even counted to 120,000?"

"A life's work," I joked.

"Exactly," Finbar said. "That's my intention. To make spiders my life's work."

We were delighted. Finbar was eleven, and we were glad to have a budding scientist in the family. I did not doubt that the boy would find a way to serve the community as usefully as I had. I returned the irrelevant book and put in an order for *Spiders and their Ways*, a fat volume which Finbar would read and reread until the pages were worn, and he knew it all by heart.

Although we were pleased with Finbar's development, we had our little worries like any parents. Alice was disappointed by the steady darkening of his blond curls, which meant that our Finbar would be black-haired after all. I was more concerned by the unusual walk that he'd developed, worried enough to consult a specialist. The boy was shuttling, sometimes even scooting sideways across a room, instead of advancing in the normal way.

The consultant proved unhelpful. He muttered something about peculiar gaits running in a family. Glancing at Finbar's face while the consultant was talking, I noticed an insolent expression that I'd never seen there before. I realised that the lad was growing up. He was becoming his own person. It occurred to me that his strange walk might be of his own design. The teenage years were upon us.

At home he rifled his wardrobe, packing most of his clothes into sacks for St Vincent de Paul. He saved a couple of black polos, a pair of black cords and a thick black jumper. "From now on," he announced, "my underwear must be black." We smiled. Alice, with her own penchant for white, was especially sympathetic. "Also, if you please, some underarm deodorant," Finbar continued. "And Mum? I need exercise tights. I want to know what there is to know about ballet."

Alice stroked his cheek with her finger. Classes were found, and Finbar immersed himself in dance. Soon he could stretch his leg over his head and bend right over backwards.

Now, when Alice and Finbar walked out together, they made a striking pair, he in black and she in white. Already, he had grown taller than she was, and although his voice was just breaking, they looked more like a couple than mother and son. Alice obviously relished his eccentric appearance as much as he did. She sewed furry ridges onto his black jumpers, ridges that resembled the hairy forelegs of a spider. She knitted him a tight-fitting cap that he wore constantly, with three sets of eye shapes stitched over its crown.

It struck me that perhaps they were too close. Not that I was jealous. Heaven forbid that a man become jealous of his own son. But I knew that Alice was not strong. Should Finbar disappoint her, it could prove a traumatic blow. I feared that in his teenage confusion, he might suddenly reject her.

The irony is that it was she who rejected him.

One afternoon when I was reading the Death Notices in the paper, Alice rushed in. "Jimmy, come quick!" she urged, her words tumbling out with uncharacteristic vigour. I followed her into the garden where Finbar was perched high in one of the oaks. I couldn't see what the excitement was about.

"Look!" she insisted. "Keep watching him."

Finbar was still. He was staring as he often did, and, even from the distance, I was aware of the deep black of his eyes. Suddenly, his arm shot out, his palm snapping shut, apparently around an insect. He peeked in at his booty, poked it with a finger, then popped it into his mouth, chewing with obvious satisfaction.

"Isn't it horrible?" Alice shuddered. "He is eating flies."

"Finbar?" I cried. "What are you doing, son?"

"Lunching." Even from the ground, we could hear his contented belch.

It was grotesque, of course, but I could see the funny side too. I interpreted it as the type of extraordinary joke that teenagers will play to annoy their parents. Alice did not see it my way. Indeed, she had turned green and was relieving herself of her own lunch in the nearby petunia bed.

In the meantime Finbar dropped to the ground on his rope, and stood before me in his exercise tights and black string vest. "Dad," he said. "I've something important to tell you."

Alice had sufficiently recovered to glance up, but as soon as she looked at his face, she was retching again.

"Wipe your mouth, son," I said. "There's a wing, or something, stuck to your lip."

Finbar's tongue flicked the offending object into his mouth. "Dad, the fact is, I'm sorry that I'm a real boy, or man, or whatever . . . I wish that I were a spider instead. All my significant inclinations are those of a spider."

I laughed out loud. His significant inclinations? I'm afraid that I didn't take the boy seriously, at least not then, but Alice did. Her almond eyes were narrowing with distaste. "I thought it was only a game," she said. Her voice was bitter with accusation.

"No, Mum," he replied, "it was the real thing." He held her gaze for a few moments, then his face relaxed, as if a great weight had been lifted from his mind. He scampered off to his bedroom, where we heard the scraping sounds of furniture being moved, and the banging of a hammer.

The next morning, when I looked in, I was astonished. The bedroom was empty save for a great orb web, woven from rope, suspended from the four walls. Finbar grinned from a position above the window, before sliding down one of the laterals to approach me, the web undulating.

"Well, Dad, what do you think?"

It was beautiful, I had to admit it. The natural colouring of the rope and wooden floor, with the light streaming through the curtainless window, created a delightfully uncluttered effect. My heart went out to the boy. He was my son and I would always love him, no matter what he did. I realised something of what it must have cost him to declare his predilection. It was not what I would have chosen for him. But if he truly longed to be a spider, then maybe I shouldn't interfere. Perhaps there was a purpose behind his behaviour, significant in some way. An idea sprang into my head and offered me some consolation: that is, that the future of the universe depends upon our offspring knowing better than we do.

I shared these thoughts with Alice, but she didn't understand. When she saw Finbar in his web, she screamed. From that moment, she refused to have anything to do with him. Finbar was at first mystified by the withdrawal of her affection and respect. Gradually, he grew sullen and reclusive. Our home which had always been such a happy place was now fraught with silent tensions.

I tried to hold everything together. Though his mother had rejected him, I had no intention of allowing Finbar to become an outcast. Although my work entails only limited contact with the public, I decided to share what there was. I invited Finbar to attend my funerals, where his penchant for black raised no eyebrows. It was not an ideal activity for the boy – or young man, as he had become – but at least it got him out and about, although I do not doubt that his presence has been instrumental in the steady falling off of my custom over the past years.

I prayed constantly that Alice might reconcile herself to Finbar's persuasion. As time passed, I never abandoned hope, all the while her aversion seemed to grow. I talked with her as I had always talked, perhaps faster, perhaps more desperately, trying to get over the awkwardness . . . but to tell you the truth, Alice rarely bothered even to look at me anymore. I was frightened. This adorable woman, whom I had always understood so well, was slipping away from me.

The crisis came on the rocky beach at Killiney, where I was struggling to be positive about our boy. "Spiders are master weavers," I argued. "They are Nature's engineers. They are actors and experts of disguise." I squeezed her hand persuasively. "Were it not for spiders, the world as we know it would fall apart."

"How is that?"

Relieved that at last I had awakened some response, I waxed eloquent. "They eat the weevils and locusts and aphids and beetles which destroy our crops. They eat the flies and mosquitoes that spread disease. Yes, every year, kilo for kilo, spiders gobble more bugs than the weight of all people on earth."

Alice pulled away her hand and wrinkled her nose. "You smell like formaldehyde," she complained. "You bore me. Yes, Jimmy, you are a fucking bore."

I was too shocked to protest. Her almond eyes glinted like knives.

"Our son revolts me," she continued. "In one sick moment, we created him together. I have paid the price ever since. Jimmy, you revolt me too." She turned away, wandering back towards the car on her own.

I was hurt. Who wouldn't be? But even then, I didn't give up. I, who so rarely mixed business with pleasure, thought of Horace. Isn't that astonishing? The irony amuses me even now, here in my workroom, as I palpate her lifeless face, kneading and stroking it, striving to do my best as always. Yes, I brought Horace into the heart of our household, and he in a heightened emotional state after his wife's death from cancer. I might as well have thrown water onto a burning chip pan.

My intentions were excellent. I knew that Alice would admire Horace's Edwardian suits and his taste for mature wines. I liked him myself for his ready observations on the human condition. My hope was that the presence of an outsider would pull Alice out of her shell and bring back the happy days of our past. With hindsight, I understand that I introduced Horace precisely at the moment when Alice was ready to leave me.

I realised what I'd done when I overheard them giggling on the sofa. I crept up behind them. They were whispering. I came closer. I heard Horace say, "I could scoop you up in my hand."

I'm still very fond of Horace. It's impossible to dislike a man with a moustache that droops down to his chin before curling up into a winged smile. Making no scenes, I bowed to the inevitable. With tears in my eyes, I watched Alice wrap up her shoes, pair by pair, in fine white tissue paper. She looked through me as though I weren't there. Already her eyes were focused on Horace. I helped pack her things into Horace's car. I even wished them well.

I am no pathologist, yet I know why Alice took her own life. Poor Horace. A gentleman of his ilk must feel so guilty, although it wasn't his fault. He wasn't to know that such a natural act could push his fragile partner over the edge. I have laid Alice out. My professional eye has recognised the secretions and noted the bruises, which suggest that Horace did not repress his manly urges like I did. Yes, sex reared its head during Alice's last hours, shattering her pretty illusion that her new relationship would remain as unstained as ours had become.

Poor Alice. She didn't have a realistic view of life at all. When she arrived in my workroom, she didn't look a bit like herself. They never do, not when the death has been violent, especially when poison's been involved. Her mouth was twisted, her eyebrows wrenched out of position and her nostrils hideously flared. According to Horace, she drank the poison out of a white china cup.

When I saw how bad she was, I wasn't sure that I could do her justice. Funny. All the while I've been working on her, I've felt that Finbar was here. Ready to jump in and say that I had it wrong, that the pose wasn't naturalistic. I swear that I heard his boy's voice piping clearly in my head, just like it used to.

At any rate, I've got her now. This is Alice at her best, her face smooth and calm, her body swathed in white. If you'll pardon my vanity, perhaps she looks even more beautiful. Optimist that I am, I never gave up hope, not even after she left me. I dreamed that she'd come back, that we'd have another child, a brother or a sister for Finbar. Alice wasn't old. Today they think nothing of having kiddies in their forties.

I'm nearly ready now, only waiting for Finbar to telephone. Such a good boy, Finbar, he wouldn't dream of turning up without permission, though I never refuse it.

He sidles down the church path, dramatic in black. He lurks in the back of the church, listening, taking the service in with watchful eyes. The casket is borne out, the mourners file past, the church is quite empty. Then Finbar lets loose. He flies across the pew backs, dancing on all fours, launching himself at the pulpit, leaping down again, back and forth with dazzling agility, wriggling his behind, secreting yards and yards of imaginary silk, spinning a vast web over the empty church. I have seen it often, but still it fascinates.

There are not many fathers who can boast that they always know where their sons are.

I have rolled the oak casket alongside my worktable. I am lifting Alice in onto her bed of silk. She is light as a feather. The casket is eighteen inches wide and twelve inches deep. There is plenty of room.

I would like to lie down beside her. It isn't right that she should be alone. She was never strong. I feel as close to her now as ever I did, perhaps even closer. But I must fight back my inclinations. I can't walk out on my responsibilities. Somebody has got to look after Finbar. Any moment now, the phone is going to ring.

My Mother's Daughter

"You're late," my mother says sharply, tapping the toe of her neat shoe upon the linoleum floor.

I am not late. When it comes to my mother, I take particular care to arrive at the agreed hour, but I feel defensive nonetheless. She looks me over from head to foot. Although faded by age to a watery blue, her eyes retain their power to strike me with a sudden breathlessness, and all my inadequacies, both real and imaginary, bubble to the surface.

"That dress is too young for you, Polly," she says. "One of your daughters should be wearing that dress."

My three young daughters refuse to accompany me on these visits, but I don't press the issue. Perhaps I don't like them to see me through my mother's eyes.

Her handbag waits on the bed, an exquisite relic of the 1940s, brocaded and elegant, its ebony handle gleaming. With a vigour extraordinary for her years, my mother flings herself into her coat.

"And how is Victor?" she demands, not waiting for the answer as she bustles out of her room. I trot after her as though I were a child again. "When people ask after me," she says, "tell them the truth, Polly. Always tell them the truth. Explain how you've put me into a cage and thrown away the key. I don't know how you can sleep at night, knowing what you've done to me."

It is six months now since my mother signed herself into the nursing home, before informing her few surviving acquaintances that I'd done the dirty on her. I overheard her on the telephone, basking in the badness of her thankless daughter. "Sharper than a serpent's tooth," she enthused, wielding her most thrilling tones. "What can you expect? You give up your life for them, then they dump you into the old people's home."

My mother is a very dramatic lady. Indeed, nearly a lifetime ago, she played Juliet at the Gate Theatre.

I follow her down the green and yellow corridor towards the lift. In spite of her bad hips, her bearing is regal. The fine black cloth of her coat billows about her ankles like a coronation robe. It is impossible not to admire her. I have always admired her and would have been glad of her admiration in return.

"I am like a caged beast in this place," she says.

"There is nothing stopping you from moving out. They're building new flats near Seapoint."

"Hah!" she snorts. "Flats are for yuppies. Besides, there are not enough people about the place in a flat." She bows her head, taking an imaginary curtain call before an imaginary audience.

The corridor smells, that tang peculiar to nursing homes of cabbage and disinfectant and urine. Sometimes at night, when I'm on my way out to a film or to a party, ready to have a good time, that smell rushes out from nowhere, burrowing up my nostrils and fogging my head. It clings to my clothes, staining the fabric of my evening with its melancholy.

The long corridor snakes around the corner, where the double windows let in a flood of light. In the recess, half a dozen wheelchairs are congregated, cradling the oldest and least competent inhabitants of the nursing home, a tidy row of ancient women and men, blankets tucked around them as they dribble and doze and stare.

"Just look at them," my mother sniffs. "Old bats! I ask you, what does a woman like me have in common with the likes of them? In themselves, they are an unanswerable argument for euthanasia."

If they hear her in their wheelchairs, they don't react.

"Old bats!" she repeats, a shade louder, then she grins, clicking her teeth.

Out the windows you can see Bulloch Harbour and the bay. A cloud passes, its purple shadow skimming over the green sea below. I have often watched that beautiful sea from other vantage points, watched it glimmer and swirl from blue to green to grey, then back again. All of a sudden, I grab the nearest wheelchair, swinging it around so that its aged occupant faces the water.

"And just what do you think you're doing, Polly?" my mother demands.

"Why shouldn't they look out instead of in?"

Her lips curl into a lemony smile. "You dare-devil you. If the nurse catches you, she'll eat you."

But I swing all the wheelchairs around, just the same. "Hurry on," my mother says, "you are too sentimental for words. No doubt you'd play Beethoven to them, if you got the chance."

My mother brushes an empty crisp packet off the passenger seat before she sits into my car. "I didn't let you eat crisps," she says, "not when you were your daughters' age. It will give them spots."

Cautiously, I pull out into the Ulverton Road.

"Of course, I should have drowned you in a bucket when you were born," she adds reflectively. "That's what they do with unwanted kittens."

I am accustomed to her saying things like this. Most of the time, I try to believe that she doesn't mean them maliciously, that it's just her way of communicating.

At difficult moments you need to be pleasant, my husband Victor says. So I think pleasant thoughts about home and my work and my daughters.

"I was forty-two years of age when you were born," my mother says. "The same age that you are now. It was a ridiculous age for calving, the single undignified episode in my entire lifetime."

I concentrate on the road. As I turn onto the Blackrock bypass, a few substantial drops of rain splatter onto the windscreen.

"You never fetch me out of my cage on a sunny day,"

31

my mother says. "Yesterday, the sun shone all day. You should have come yesterday."

She snaps open her brocaded handbag, taking out a nail file. Her fingernails are still the perfect red ovals that I remember from my childhood. I used to wonder at those perfect shapes, longing to become a woman like her.

In fact, I have not turned out badly. I work in biological research, and my opinions about viruses and related creepy-crawlies are chronicled from time to time by the media. Victor and I get on well together, and our rearing of our children, if not exactly seamless, has so far avoided major disaster. Three peas in a pod: that's what my mother calls my daughters, reflecting unfavourably upon how they resemble their father.

As we approach the city centre, the traffic slows to a crawl. My mother is growing impatient. "I hope that you won't park too far away. Last time, I got a blister on my instep from the distance that you made me walk."

Since the Drury Street car park is full, I settle for a double yellow line, praying without conviction for mercy from the traffic wardens. I don't blame my mother for impatience. At the age of eighty-four, I expect that I'll be impatient too.

In Bewley's she marches back through the crowd towards the plush seats under the stained glass windows, while I queue for coffee and sticky buns. By the time that I join her, she is daubing at her eyes with a handkerchief. "This isn't the way that it used to be," she complains. "There were waitresses then, and the almond buns actually tasted of almonds."

I remember it well, my mother in her prime, whooshing past the tables in full sail, dazzling in her red cape and impossibly tall fur hat. Heads turned for her then, and the air buzzed with excited recognition. But nobody knows my mother anymore. I understand that it's not absent waitresses or inferior buns that have brought the tears to her old eyes. My heart aches, but I know better than to offer comfort. She would only brush me away.

"So," she says brusquely, "tell me something interesting, Polly. Impress me."

There is no point in talking about my research, towards which she manifests a studied indifference. So I rattle on about my daughters, their enthusiasms and loathings, their flute lessons and mathematical prizes. I suspect that my mother is listening, even though her eyes sweep round and round the tea room. She smooths her hair with a stagey gesture. The huge diamond still glitters on her hand, only her fingers have gone bony, and the loose ring has polished the skin beneath with its weight. I remember that hand, taut-skinned and plump, buttering bread, spreading the jam as thickly as any child could desire. I remember those eyes, laughing and loving me. I remember loving my mother so much that the very possibility of her going away, or dying, filled me with the blackest of terrors. Perhaps she was really not so bad a mother as she lets on to have been.

A girl passes our table in a flapping dress, unbuttoned

from hem to crotch, exposing lavender tights and heavy black shoes. "And she thinks she looks gorgeous," my mother sniffs. "You used to do things like that to me, Polly. You shamed me with your vulgar clothing. Not to mention those misfits that you fell in love with. I'll never forget that dreadful what's-his-name from Crumlin, the one whose eyes moved in opposite directions."

I smile brightly at my mother, pretending that I feel no pain, but I'm glad – just the same – that our coffee is drunk and it's time to go.

She is quiet for most of the journey back, melted into the passenger seat, every muscle relaxed. It is the way she often behaves, as if reserving her energies for her next performance. Suddenly she pulls herself upright. "What I resent the most about you, Polly," she says softly, "is how happily you married. Your father was such a peasant. He never had what I wanted, not when I wanted it."

Cautiously I glance at her. It's a possibility I've never considered before: that she might be envious. She glints at me like a sea bird about to devour a sprat. Then I remember a day trip, twenty years in the past, when she tried to cajole Victor, then my fiancé, into marrying another girl. I shiver once again at this treachery.

Her timing impeccable, my mother attacks. "When I was growing up, we had a maid named Polly. She was an ignorant Welsh girl. I named you after her."

I can't take anymore. I pull the wheel hard, turning the corner into the nursing home drive so fast that the gravel spits under my tyres. I speed recklessly through the narrow stone archway into the car park. I jump out. The passenger door creaks open. I am counting the seconds now.

We drag through reception into the lift. My mother has begun to smile. She is looking younger than her eighty-four years, and somehow radiant. I follow her into her room. "I'm feeling quite refreshed now," she says. "You'd be surprised how I look forward to our little encounters."

My chest is tight. My head is thumping. I brush my lips against her stiff cheek. Not bothering with the lift I flee down the stairs, out, out into the sea air. I barely make it to the car before the tears come, cascading down my cheeks. With shaking hands, I light the single cigarette of my week and I smoke, inhaling with great gasps through my tears.

After a while, I blow my nose and mop my cheeks. Then, with supreme effort, I square my shoulders and become myself again, Polly McKenna, the capable woman created by my failed efforts to dazzle my mother, the woman that other people know and respect. And once again, I am no longer my mother's daughter. At least not for another week.

Seduced

"Oh, Vincent O'Toole," she says, "it's magic the way the stars twinkle down upon us."

You can see the stars, here and there, through the crumbling roof of the derelict warehouse he calls home and studio. They lie, Calley and Vincent, companionable strangers on his straw mattress, where the fluttering of her body has made him drowsy.

"Oh, Vincent O'Toole," she says, "I love you so much," and she locks her slender leg over his substantial thigh.

"So much?" he teases. He doesn't believe Calley since he scarcely knows her. Instead he seizes a fistful of her dark curls, admiring the way that they bounce back into shape when he lets go. Resilient, he thinks. It's a word he likes.

"Beliefs are important," she says. "I believe that every star in the sky has the soul of a baby." Her eyes glow like mother-of-pearl in the dark, but he's too sleepy to notice. "So many stars," she whispers, "so many babies."

"Why don't we talk in the morning?" Vincent O'Toole turns over and falls asleep. Together they float in a sea of shadows and space, watched over by the hulking outlines of Vincent's possessions.

When the morning light has flooded the warehouse, Vincent reaches for the woman, but next to him the mattress has gone cold. Without getting up, he peers among the canvases and buckets and plastic sheeting, between the tyres and silvery sand, the sieves and barrows and bins, the trunks and rusty trolleys, throughout the jungle of homeless objects that he collects for his art. Improbably Calley spots him first, alert to his darting eye. "Vincent," she calls. Her voice pipes like birdsong among the bright treasures. There she is, enthroned upon an armchair, a striking figure in her red Indian dress splashed over the green brocade, a heady display of colour and texture. Her black curls tumble about her gaunt face and shoulders. As he looks, he sees a Florentine madonna, transported from the fourteenth century. But wait. Something is askew in the image. Her skinny elbows bob like a chicken flapping its wings.

"What the hell are you doing?" he inquires.

"Knitting."

"What the hell for?"

"Our baby."

Vincent laughs, his morning crankiness quite

dispelled by this whimsy. The idea of himself as a father is ludicrous.

He bounces up, bull-keen to tackle the day, and washes with rainwater from a bucket. As he slaps the cold water onto his chest, he stands astride, his huge thighs glistening, a colossus in his warehouse; and he tells Calley his story about the farmer and the three-legged chicken. It's a good laugh, Vincent's story, but she isn't amused.

He is not put out. The girls he brings home are all sorts, and he doesn't give a damn for their sense of humour. It was last night that he picked Calley up. He'd nearly squashed her, a frail insect, as she'd hovered on the footpath outside his local. He'd thought she was a child, but when she turned her plaintive face full upon him, he'd seen a waif-woman with an enigmatic smile, so he'd invited her back to share his roof for the night. Why shouldn't he? Was he not Vincent O'Toole, Saviour, Superman and Healer of Strays?

"Well, Calley," he says now in his best cowboy drawl, "I am going to rustle you up some breakfast." She inclines her head towards him, but she keeps on knitting. This knitting irritates him. Who ever saw a madonna knit? "If you have to knit," he suggests, "knit something useful. Socks for instance." He imagines a mountain of socks, a huge fluffy mound of startling colours. "Yes," he tells her, "make me some socks. Something bizarre. Something amusing. Why not orange socks?"

"When I finish this baby jacket," she answers, flapping her elbows.

"Baby jacket," he mutters. "Pah!" He retreats from its horrible pinkness into his beloved larder. Behind a partition, he has refashioned the country store of his boyhood. He believes in quantities of preserved food as a declaration of faith in tomorrow. He intends never to run out. His tins are stacked densely upon the shelves. Tin after tin, loyal soldiers, labels spattered with damp, yellowing from age. Stew and corned beef and peas. Beans galore. Pear halves, pineapple pieces and smiling mandarin segments. Bottles of beer and tomato sauce. Enormously happy in his larder, Vincent begins to sing.

"In the town where I was born
Lived a man who sailed the sea . . . "

He taps out the rhythm as he lights his battered bottled gas cooker.

Into the skillet go the sausages, snip, snip, snip. Plump as a fat lady's fingers, they shiver and jump, mingling juices with the hot oil. The smell makes Vincent salivate. With a flourish, he cracks the eggs.

"And he told us of his life
In the land of submarines."

The yellowy egg hearts throb in the whitening albumen and Vincent's stomach rumbles. Contentedly, he hacks blood purple wedges from a loop of black pudding.

As he cooks, he dreams of painting Calley. Calley in a panorama of monster lorries, meat hooks, carcasses and smashed aircraft. Calley, his stray from a Florentine fresco, overwhelmed by technology. Calley, sacrificed on the altar of modern machinery.

Delighted with his idea, Vincent ladles breakfast onto two plates. By now he is ravenous. His inspiration knits in the green brocade chair. He studies her with pride in his plans for her. "It's ready," he cries, exhilarated by his power. He slaps the plates down on the trestle table. But Calley is slow to join him.

"I can't paint without a good breakfast," he complains. She rises ever so slowly, Calley from the sea, wafting towards him on a scallop shell. She strolls over. He is amazed to see her knit while she walks, her bony little fingers speeding back and forth, in and out. Faster than a croupier counting money with an agile forefinger. Bony but steely.

She is nearly at the table. Vincent sits, seizing his own knife and fork. She stands beside him, so slight of stature that her face is barely above his.

"I can't eat this junk," she says.

"Pardon?"

She slops his cup of tea into a rainwater bucket. "I'm doing you a favour," she says. "D'you know what's in it? Tannic acid. That junk would atrophy your insides. And you an artist. You should be ashamed of using stimulants. Did Leonardo da Vinci need stimulants? Of course not. He didn't want his insides to turn into old shoe leather."

Vincent stares at her mouth. He wonders at the extravagance of words pouring from such ethereal lips. His fried eggs are going cold. "Sit down and eat your breakfast," he grumbles. "We'll talk later."

Calley stamps her little foot. "Have you considered the fat content in that lot? If it congeals on the plate, what's it going to do to your arteries? Do you want to poison the baby?"

"What baby?"

"Our baby. Of course it's still only a cell or two," she adds reflectively.

"What are you talking about?"

"You know what I'm talking about."

She wasn't serious. She couldn't be. How could her sparrow-like frame serve something so vigorous as real motherhood? "Besides," as Vincent adds out loud, "we only did it once."

"You only *need* to do it once. Any teenager knows that. Only we're not teenagers. At least you're not." She smiles sweetly before continuing. "I selected you as father because I like your painting and because I want our daughter to be an artist too. But I think you should try sculpture. You'd be good at it. I appreciate that the critics detest your work now, but fashions change, and my belief is that some day you'll be famous . . . And, oh yes, naturally, I hope we'll do it more than once."

Vincent stares incredulously. "Just how do you know? How *could* you know that you're . . . well, that it took."

"I know." She presses her palms solemnly upon her abdomen.

"Hold on!" Vincent snaps. "There is no baby! There couldn't be!" The vast space of the warehouse begins to wobble about him.

"A love child," Calley says.

Sweat dribbles down Vincent's neck. "This is crazy. If I'd thought you weren't on the pill, I wouldn't have . . ."

But Calley interrupts. "Love children aren't like ordinary children," she says. "I read about them in a book. Our little girl will be remarkable."

The warehouse is now spinning around Vincent, a kaleidoscope of colour and shape. He grabs a cold sausage and bolts it, feeling its nourishment flow down into his stomach.

Calley watches him chew. "Fat men die younger," she says.

Flinging his plate to the floor, he rages like a bear. "I don't like this!" he yells. "What's more, I don't believe it. You've got to be crazy! Besides you've made me lose my temper. If there's anything I can't stand, it's losing my temper. I am going out now. When I come back you'd better be gone."

As he flees Calley's voice pursues him. "You're overemotional. Even shocked. But everything's going to be all right."

Ignoring her, he flings himself out, squeezing past the barricaded door, trampling through the overgrown yard, for once not caring who might see him. He kicks his way through stink weed and couch grass. In his path, a brick glints, pink like a snake's eye midst the dandelions. He heaves it back at his squat, watching it float in an arc towards one of the high windows. The glass shatters with a satisfying crash, and he hears the debris tinkling down among his things.

"Aroint thee, witch!" he bellows, shaking his fist. "Away! Be gone when I come back!"

He hopes that he has frightened her. Outrageous

insect! Had he plucked her out of the gutter to be insulted? To have his breakfast spoiled? To be violated? The woman was mad. "Some madonna," he snarls. "The devil's own!" Roughly he squares his shoulders, determined to shake her out of his head.

The Grand Canal shimmers before him. He begins to walk, snorting the air hard into his lungs. His elbows pump, sharp and fast. Power walking. His sandals slip and slide. His face turns red. Runners, he thinks. I'd better get myself some runners. In no time at all he remembers how hungry he is. Tousle-haired and panting, he bursts into a shop so tiny that his prodigious bulk fills it entirely.

Behind the counter, the elderly shopkeeper shies away from him, rat-eyed with terror. "Take it! Take every penny!" he squeals, his yellow lips aquiver, his hands tearing the drawer out of an ancient cash register, to dump its contents on the counter.

Vincent inspects the pile of dog-eared notes and coppers. "I don't want your money," he says. "All I want is some bread and a bottle of lemonade."

The old man shudders. His bulbous nose twitches.

"What's the matter with you?" Vincent asks. "I don't have two heads. Aren't you going to serve me?"

"You mean you're not one of them hooligans?"

"Pardon?"

"Them mingy little rotters that did me last week."

"The swine."

Relieved, the old man retrieves his money. Then he pulls up his vest. "Look at this, Mister," he says.

The sagging torso is blue-black with bruises, pitted as if gravel had been ground into it. In his head Vincent hears the thump of young fists upon old flesh. He shudders. "It's an evil world we live in," he mutters. Still, why should the geezer mistake him, Vincent O'Toole, for a batterer of old men? In some dudgeon Vincent gathers up his loaf and bottle of lemonade. He is so hungry that he tears off a handful of bread and stuffs it into his mouth.

"What did they take?" he asks, chewing.

"Everything. If I'd had a shotgun, I'd have peppered the buggers." The old man hawks, his venom-spittle shooting across the counter, but his baldy head droops onto a wheezing chest.

Vincent is fascinated. How awful it must be to grow old, he thinks. Who could consider it pleasant to share a pillow with such a moth-eaten head? Soberly Vincent delves into his pocket and pulls out a fiver. "Here," he says. "Keep the change."

A claw-like hand snatches the money. But as Vincent backs out, he sees suspicion, not gratitude, taking root on the old man's face. Doubts seethe in Vincent's mind. What's wrong with me today? Did I not bring him even a moment's happiness? Have I lost my magic touch?

"Calley," niggles a voice in the back of his head, but Vincent repudiates it.

Back in the sunshine Vincent blows the pong of advanced years out of his nose and heads for town, feasting on bread, scattering crumbs for the birds. He basks in the infinity of greens around him. Green is his favourite colour. He sees it everywhere. Green feathered upon green, emerald upon jade. He would paint the world green, if only he had a brush big enough.

On Baggot Street Bridge, Vincent eagerly inspects the bookshop window. Nothing. He pops in the door, flashing an engaging smile at the proprietor. "Fine day, Mr O'Toole," she says. Frisky old bird, he thinks. Buoyant. No chance she'd take him for a hooligan.

"Has it come in yet?" he demands.

"Remind me."

Vincent says nothing but plunges back to Poetry, where he spots the slim spine with its golden lettering. What? Only two copies? He seizes them both and rushes back to the front.

"Look here," he says. "*Green out of Chaos!* How's that for a title? Hugh Fennessy."

"Never heard of him."

"You will. Listen. This is a man with a future." The volume falls open in Vincent's hand. He reads expressively, each syllable resonant.

"Everywhere the fleshy dead
lie battered, broken, stilled;
but afterwards the fruitful worm,
earth from their flesh will till."

"Well, what do you think?" he asks.

"Purple," she chirps.

Vincent is unperturbed. "Mark my words. Everyone will be reading this Fennessy man. You'd better reorder. Get up a window display. The public will snap them up."

"Hah!"

Does he imagine it? Does her spirited eye look at him with particular interest? Has his physical presence tapped some rich memory in her silver-haired head?

"A piece of advice," he says. "Keep a copy yourself. Don't you know what a first edition of early Beckett is worth these days?"

Vincent pays for both copies and strolls out. Across the bridge he sees Bord Fáilte. "Welcome!" he cries cheerily, "welcome indeed!" "With compliments," he writes on a flyleaf. "Hugh Fennessy," he scrawls, and deposits the book in the letter box. Then Vincent O'Toole, alias Hugh Fennessy, heads jauntily for the city centre.

In the Brobdingnagian shadow of Holles Street Hospital, a behemoth-woman waits for the light. No maiden this, but a great tun of female, swollen with pregnancy. Purple veins bulge on her piano legs. Thick ankles spill out of feet in men's shoes. The light gone green, she lumbers across the road, shoving a low-riding pram that bursts with baby and toddler. Her shopping swings in a net bag, and three more youngsters, puffy-skinned and snouty, cling to her skirts. Too many children.

Vincent pulls out his notebook and begins to draw. He imagines this woman as the centre of an enormous mural, unwanted children teeming about her, nose pickers gobbling up the world's resources. He sketches quickly, staring misty-eyed at her departing rump. Suddenly he runs after her.

"Stop!" he cries. His fingers founder in the soft moist flesh of her arm.

She looks at him, too weary to be surprised.

"Good woman," he says, "I understand your plight . . . Believe me, I sympathise. Take this!" He presses the remaining copy of *Green out of Chaos* into her hand. "The next time your husband seeks to have his way with you, tell him to read this instead."

She fingers the golden lettering on the spine. Mutely she slides the book in with her shopping, next to the onions.

Vincent hurries on ahead. He feels like leaping into the air, stretching his feathery arms wide and flying like a great bird over the rooftops. Hasn't he just resolved another of life's heartaches? He plunges into Nassau Street where he greets the busload of American tourists disgorging into the college with a cheery, two-fingered salute.

In the pub it's dark and cool. Henry snaps open a newspaper between them. "I don't want to talk," he grunts.

Naturally Vincent's curiosity is aroused. He notes that Henry's fuzzy hair is sadly drooping and that his skin has gone spotty. "What's up, Henry?" he insists. "How's tricks?"

"Would you kindly piss off, Vincent."

"Tch, tch, manners . . . A behaviour unworthy of the one and only white-suited Henry Harrison. Painter of mouths *extraordinaire*. Big mouths, small mouths, mouths yelling and mouths in repose." Vincent wraps an avuncular arm about Henry's shoulders. "It should strike you as obvious, my boy, that I won't let up until you tell me what's wrong."

"All right then," Henry sighs. "It's Denise. She wants to get married. So now that you know, you can piss off."

"Married? I don't understand. You've been shacked up with her for years. Why the hell would she want to get married?"

"She says it's a question of property." Henry glares into his pint. "I own nothing anyway. She can have it all, only I don't want to get married."

"And I thought she was a sensible girl," Vincent muses, "although a trifle too full in the bosom for my taste."

"For Chrissake, what do her boobs have to do with you?"

"It's a question of aesthetics. She looks like she might tip over. Big boobs are a sign of instability in a woman."

"You're an exceedingly irritating man, Vincent. If you weren't so big, I'd thump you. If I'd known you were coming here, I'd have gone some place else."

Vincent grins. "Come on, oul' flower. I'll buy you a jar, and we'll drink to the happy day. Besides I'm sympathetic. I have woman troubles of my own."

"I'm not surprised. The way you carry on with women is disgraceful. Although what they see in you in the first place is one of life's mysteries."

"I'm loveable."

"You are in my arse. You stink, Vincent. When you sat down beside me, I knew who it was without looking."

"Rainwater. I wash in rainwater. Nothing's purer."

"For Chrissake, have you never heard of total immersion? I don't understand you. You've plenty of money, but you live like a tinker. You drag home rubbish off the streets . . ."

"Artefacts. Grist for my mill."

"Rubbish," Henry insists. "Why any woman would set foot in your place, I don't know."

"I look after a woman," Vincent says with dignity. "I make her immortal through my art."

"Yeah. Then you kiss her good-bye. You're a hypocrite."

"Hypocrite? That's hard. I am an artist."

Henry sneers. "You're a megalomaniac, Vincent, and one fine day some smart developer is going to flatten that warehouse of yours and everything that's in it. I only hope that I'll be there to watch."

"Very droll, Henry. Very fucking droll." But Vincent is uneasy. He sees Calley again, Calley on a mountain of tyres and tubing. Calley, haloed in wire and spark plugs. Only he'd rather not be thinking about her at all.

It is mid-afternoon and Vincent is not feeling his usual happy self. He peers into the window of a fishmonger's and sees a scene of carnage on crushed ice. Chopped and chunked, lumps of monk fish moulder next to cod and clammy haddock. The jaws of a sea trout gape at dead fans of ray. The silver-bellied mackerel tarnish before Vincent's eyes. Death everywhere. Furiously he begins to sketch. A netful of people takes shape under his pencil, people struggling for their lives. Why not glue fish scales to his work, Vincent thinks, and smear it all in fish blood?

The fishmonger, concerned for his custom, materialises at Vincent's shoulder. "Can I help you, sir?" he inquires with caution.

"You can," Vincent growls, without looking up. "I'll have one of each."

"One of each what, sir?"

"Are you deaf?" Vincent snarls. "One of everything you have!"

"Will I include the crustaceans and molluscs, sir, that is, one shrimp, one scallop, one mussel, one . . ."

"I said everything, didn't I?" Vincent pulls a fistful of notes out of his pocket and waves them under the fishmonger's nose.

Weighed down with oozing bags, their white plastic knotted about his fingers, Vincent strides homewards leaving a miasma of fish smell behind him. He is angry now, what with so much of his day routed and nothing accomplished. It is all Calley's fault. She, who had tracked him home to ravish him. The hell with her!

Vincent stares into the canal, where the water that shimmered in the morning now broods murkily. A metallic rod juts out from the swirling waters. Dropping his fishy bags, Vincent slides down the bank, wading out into the quagmire. The treasure shudders beneath his mighty heavings. Suddenly, with a great squelch, tattered leatherette breaks loose from the mud, floating to the surface of the yellowy-brown water.

"A pram!" he cries. His dripping discovery totters, its hood gone, a wheel missing, its box-like body that of a coffin. He strips the slime and weed away with his bare hands. Fate, he realises, has sent him this pram for his Malthusian mural of unwanted children. He can picture his behemoth-woman shambling behind it, at one with its stink of rotten leaves and dead dogs.

As he works he hears a pathetic mewling. A scabby kitten quivers on top of his bags of fish. She claws frantically at the plastic film, an insurmountable barrier to her cat-heart's desire. He can help her, Vincent O'Toole, Saviour and Superman. He tears open a bag with his teeth, spilling out the meaty flesh of a salmon. "Good pussy," he says, as she gorges. His heart fills with affection for the tiny creature.

He flings the remaining bags into the pram. Hoisting the kitten in his great paw of a hand, Vincent arranges her tenderly on a bed of plastic and fish, where she writhes in ecstasy. Then, dragging the three-wheeled pram after him, Vincent shuffles homeward, the words of his favourite song drifting away into the fading light.

"As we live a life of ease,
Every one of us has all he needs:
Sky of blue and sea of green,
In our yellow submarine . . . "

Behind him, he leaves a trail of sludge and water like a monster snail.

Vincent stands beneath his crumbling roof, the roof through which you can see the stars. Calley is still there, but there is no more reason to fear her. She has laid herself out upon the trestle table. She has draped herself in a sheet. Juliet on a tombstone. Her head reposes upon the pink brick. He imagines the dagger in her heart, its hilt spangled with gemstones. Dead by her own hand, strewn with pansies and rosemary, her curly hair cascading over the brick.

His eyes brim with tears, but he takes his sketchbook and begins to draw. It is the least he can do. Poor mad thing. He hunches his shoulders and hums. His toes jig. With a vibrant pencil, he catches cheekbone and marble eyelids; the undulating lines of breast, abdomen and thigh; her dainty feet, each milky toe opalescent in the candlelight.

And as he draws, line by line, he comes to believe in his daughter who will never be. He finishes the drawing and admires it. If only, he thinks . . . then stops. There are straws in life that can be seized only once.

Hungry again, Vincent slips out to his larder but finds no consolation there. His storehouse has been vandalised. The blank shelves mock him, stripped by her hand, their naked wood marked with hollow rings. His buttress against tomorrow smashed. His breath comes in short, hard gasps which echo off the empty shelves.

The nearly empty shelves. Disorientated, perhaps hallucinating, Vincent sees a bag of lentils and a carton of carrot juice. Shaking his fist, he throws back his head and roars, addressing his maker. "Why have You done this to me, God? I've always served You in my own way. Are You laughing at me?" Vincent trembles. He hears a rattling sound and sees the empty shelves dancing before him like bones. He realises that even he can't live forever and that when he's gone, he will leave nothing behind.

"Would You like a glass of carrot juice, God?" he says out loud.

Laughing sardonically, he returns to Calley. His madonna entombed. Through death she has scratched her mark upon him. She, who had mounted him like a butterfly, was strong in ways of which he'd never dreamed.

In the coffin-shaped pram the kitten is stirring. Soon she leaps out, cocky now with her bellyful of fish. She pads across the warehouse floor to curvet up onto Calley's breast where she coils, purring like a full-fed lioness.

Vincent considers the kitten with melancholy eyes. It seems indecent, this intimacy between life and death. Gently he lays his hand upon her warm, furry body. Calley's eyes flutter open. "You've brought me a kitten," she says. "Why that's lovely, Vincent." She sits up, stretches, then cuddles the kitten in her lap. "I like the pram," she says.

Startled, Vincent draws back. Is she real or is he dreaming? His hand stretches out and brushes against her throat.

"I love you, Vincent," she says. "I love you so much. What a delightful little family we are going to make."

Family? Thoughtfully he squeezes her dark curls between his fingers. Her breath is warm against his cheek.

Her wiry arm emerges from the sheet that covers her. "Aren't these what you wanted?"

He accepts the orange socks from her hand, then sits beside her on the table. Kicking off his ruined sandals, he pulls the socks that she's knitted for him onto his oversized feet.

Words

On the day that Vincent came to our house, the grown-ups used a lot of words that I didn't understand. "Eponymous," Vincent said. "If there's any word I can't tolerate, it's eponymous." He was sitting close to my Mam on the green sofa. I was admiring his feet on which he wore sandals and raggy orange socks. I knew that Vincent was an artist who made big metal statues, like you'd see in a park or in front of an office block.

"Eponymous," Mammy repeated. Then she laughed, the old way that I'd nearly forgotten. The way that she used to laugh at Dad when he'd said something clever. But Dad was sitting on the floor at the other end of the room, talking to my baby brother, Luke. Luke was flat on his tummy and Dad was trying to get him to lift his head.

"C'mon fella, you can do it," my father said. "Up Luke! Up fella, up!"

"Don't talk to him like a dog," Mammy said.

Dad barked. His face was all red and happy, the way it

gets at a football match. "Up fella, up!" The baby thrashed about, hammering his little fists on the floor. It didn't look to me like he was making much progress.

Besides, I was more interested in Vincent and my Mam. "I don't like babies much," she was saying, her mouth a smiling crescent of the lipstick she hadn't worn for ages.

"Mewlers and pukers," Vincent said. He was a huge bear of a man with little gold glasses and long hair that grew out from the sides of his head, leaving a big shiny patch in the centre, where no hair grew at all.

"Eponymous," I said silently to myself. I liked the way it was different from any word I'd heard before. Why had Vincent said it twice if he liked it so little? Why had Mammy laughed her special laugh like the singing of a bird?

"A relationship's got to be give and take," she was saying. "Most women give, give, give. Then they get bitter when they get nothing back." The top part of her body leaned towards Vincent as she spoke. "I hate a bitter woman," she said. "Women have got to control themselves better." She looked smashing there on the green sofa in her flowery dress, her best dress with the roses twisting down its front. Her fingers danced and her eyes sparkled, and her voice sounded like a pocketful of coins. "I'm learning how to take what I want," she said softly, half closing her eyes and stretching like a cat.

I liked Vincent because his head was shiny and because he wore worn-out orange socks. I liked Vincent because he'd cheered Mammy up when Dad and I didn't

BRIDGE STREET BOOKS

WICKLOW TOWN

THE IRISH TIMES

Winner of

The **Best Bookshop** in Ireland

Thank you for shopping with us

Phone: (0404) 62240

info@bridgestreetbooks.ie

www.bridgestreetbooks.ie

know how. A while back she'd been all roundy like a pear on two sticks. Pregnant was the word they used for having a baby inside you. When Mammy had Luke inside her, she'd bite the head off you if you asked for anything, even a piece of bread and jam.

"Eponymous," Vincent had said. You could like or not like a person, but how could you not like a word?

With a great grunt the baby heaved his head up and gawked about like a turtle. "Great boy!" my Dad yelled. Then the baby's head thumped down and he began to bawl. I didn't like it when the baby was bawling, but Dad didn't mind. Ever. Dad just scooped him up and folded him against his jumper so you could hardly see him. "There's a fella," he crooned. "A great little fighter."

"There are plenty of words that I can't stand," Mammy said. "Effete, for one." She kind of jerked her head towards Dad, but she was looking at Vincent. "Don't you agree?" she added softly. "It's a bore." Then she smiled, her crescent lipstick smile, and her hand moved out in front of her. She was wearing her rings. Her rings with the hard stones and funny names. Sapphires and amethysts, she called them. I liked the way their colours flashed as her hand floated through the air to touch Vincent.

"What does effete mean?" I asked.

"Ah Jimmy," my mother said in a different voice, "don't ask so many questions."

"But I want to know," I insisted.

"Why don't you go out and play," she said without looking at me, "and not be always staring at a body?"

It was true. I liked to watch her. I wanted to watch her now, but Vincent was looking at me in a way that made me not like him anymore. His hands rested heavily on his thighs. They were big, square hands, all browny coloured. He looked at me as if I were the kind of beetle you might find under a flowerpot, and his big hands twitched.

I retreated to the other end of the room and my Dad.

"Dad," I began. But Dad's eyes were shining down on the baby wriggling against his front.

"Isn't he the gorgeous little fella?" he asked.

"He's OK. What does it mean, Dad?"

"What does what mean?"

"Effete?"

"Sure, your Dad wouldn't have a clue." Mammy's voice cut suddenly across the room.

I heard the rudeness but Dad didn't backtalk her. Instead he took out his handkerchief and mopped some dribble off the baby's chin. I decided I wouldn't ask him again.

Later, after Vincent had gone, we sat at the table, Dad and me and Luke in his highchair. Mammy slapped the stew and potatoes onto our plates before slumping into her chair. Dad squashed up a bit of potato and fed it to the baby. Mammy just sat there watching. I wanted her to laugh like she'd done before, but all she did was stare at Dad fussing over the baby. "You're frighteningly good at that," she snarled suddenly. Then she began to cry.

I went up to my room and lay on the bed. I could hear their voices through the floor.

"It was your idea," she said, "I didn't want it. Filthy little infant," she said. "I finished with that eight years ago."

"You'll get used to him," he said. "Give it time."

"Parasite!" she shouted. "He's a parasite! And you? You're so dumb you don't even know you're alive!" Then she began to cry again, only worse this time, great heaving sobs that went on and on. I wanted to go down and tell her it was OK, but I didn't know what was wrong. And I was afraid. I didn't want her to shout at me too.

"Parasite," I said to myself. Then I turned over and went to sleep.

In the morning she was gone. I knew from the moment that I opened my eyes and heard the awful quiet in the house. But I got up as usual. I put on the clothes that she'd left on the radiator to be warm for me. Downstairs Dad was giving the baby his bottle.

"Aren't you going to work?" I asked.

"Eat your breakfast," Dad said. "I have to mind Luke."

I poked at my porridge with the spoon already set on the table. I didn't want to let go of the spoon that she'd touched, now that she was gone. It was so quiet in the kitchen that the tick of the clock sounded loud.

Dad burped the baby and put him in his highchair. "I know you're upset, Jimmy," he said, "but it's worse for Luke. It's harder on him. A baby needs its Mam."

I looked at Luke. He was singing a little song and banging his hand on the tray in front of him. He looked the same as he did yesterday. He didn't look like he needed anybody. But Dad's face had gone all grey-coloured, and I felt a terrible sickness inside me.

"Where has she gone, Dad?"

Dad was picking at his sleeve, rolling bits of fluff between his fingers. "I don't know," he said. Then he stopped and looked at me. "She's gone to find herself."

You could hunt out a lost toy or a set of keys, I thought, and you might find them. But how could a person go about finding themselves? The word that I'd heard the night before jumped into my head. "Dad?" I asked, "what's a parasite?"

"A parasite? Why it's a thing that lives off something else. Like a flea lives off a dog by sucking its blood."

I put my spoon down then. I watched Luke in his highchair, his little fingers messing in his porridge.

I went to school, but when I came home things were worse. "Dad," I said, "they told me at school that she's gone off with Vincent. I kicked a boy for saying it."

"You shouldn't have kicked him," Dad said. "I've made you a burger."

"I'm not hungry." I tried to find Dad's eyes with mine, but he was looking out the window.

"You shouldn't have kicked him," Dad said slowly, "because it's true."

I thought of Mammy in her best dress with the roses. "Why would she do a thing like that?" I asked. I remembered Vincent's big, browny-coloured hands. I couldn't imagine Mammy putting up with those hands. She always gave out when my hands were mucky. She washed her own with a heart-shaped soap that smelled of strawberries.

The baby began to bawl.

Suddenly I was angry. "It's his fault," I yelled. "He's a parasite! I hate him! I hate Luke!"

"You don't mean that," Dad said. "You don't hate your brother."

"I do, I do!" I yelled. "It's all his fault." I picked up the plate that was waiting in my place and threw it. It shattered with a bang and the tomato sauce made a great crescent smear on the wall.

Dad was quieting the baby. I stood there, looking at the mess and waiting to be smacked. But after Dad had put the baby back in his chair, he didn't seem mad. "It's nobody's fault," he said eventually. "Anyway, it's not Luke's fault. It's just the way things are."

I looked at the crescent smear on the wall and saw my mother's red mouth smiling at Vincent. I listened to the tinkle of the broken plate as my Dad cleared it up. I felt sorry then, and began to help him.

"That's a good boy, Jimmy," he said. "It's you and me, now."

I saw that he was crying. I'd never seen my Dad crying before. I didn't know that men could cry. I put my arms around his middle and he stroked my head. We listened to the wind outside and the gurgling of the baby.

At night, when I lie in my bed, I hear the swish of her dressing-gown, and the sweet smell of strawberry soap tickles my nose. But when I get up to look for her, there's nobody there.

Happy Delivery

The manila envelope waits for me in the letterbox, as I waddle down the stairs. When I pick it up, I can feel a book inside, but the blank face of the envelope gives away no secrets. I tear it open reluctantly. I have never liked surprises. The volume is weathered and tatty like something from the stalls in front of Greene's Bookshop. The word MARY is written in faint gold lettering on the mottled cover, so I know there is no mistake. The book is intended for me.

My house is modern and my furniture is new. I do not care for old things. I feel queasy, ready to drop the book in case an insect, or worse, crawls out. But when it falls open in my hand, I see that passages have been neatly marked out with a fluorescent pink highlighter, incongruous on the yellowing pages.

This is what I read.

April 1555. Mary, Queen of England, has retired to Hampton Court Palace for her confinement. Her turbulent troubled past has been left behind at last. How happy she is! New life frolics within her royal person. A little lion! A brave homunculus! Yes, God has put buds on the trees and a baby in the Queen's belly. God, with the corporal assistance of Philip of Spain. How Mary worships the young Spanish King! For years, she anticipated his intimate touch. A patient virgin, she waited until her teeth were long in her gums, and the flames of her red Tudor hair died back into mousy brown. For Mary was ten years old when young Philip was born. Now he is twenty-eight and cock of the walk, a virile king for a queen's bedchamber.

Mary knows why God has made her wait. He has wanted her to lie alone until her womb hungered, until it clamoured, until, voracious, it sucked in Philip's seed to mingle fruitfully with her own. For Mary knows that it is no ordinary babe that flourishes in her womb. It is an infant chosen by God to drive the false faith out of England forever.

Some joke. I snap the book closed, raising a puff of dust which makes me sneeze. I sling the book onto the kitchen table and plug in the percolator. That's the worst of being pregnant. It has left me open, not only to jokes in questionable taste, but to all kinds of gossip and innuendo. My mother gloated when I told her, and it wasn't because she had long since abandoned her hopes of my making her a grandmother.

"That will put an end to your gallop, Marie," she said, sniffing curiously, "who's the father?"

If only she knew.

Max. I can't help but smile when I think about Max. He was young enough to be my son. Or nearly.

"You've had too much fun all these years," my mother complained. "You've done exactly what you wanted to do. It wasn't the same for us."

I know what she meant. I had reached adulthood at precisely the right time for a woman in Ireland. When I was growing up, I had but one ambition: not to end up like my mother. After college, I had vague intentions of wandering through Europe, living hand to mouth and drinking in life like wine. But I never got around to it. Instead I fell in love with work and getting ahead, and the rest is history.

Until . . .

I open the book and read some more, my eye drawn irresistibly to the pink highlights of turgid prose.

Mary waits, her jewelled fingers stroking her bulging abdomen. She waits for the happy delivery of her child and heir. Buzzing about her are an army of midwives, two wet nurses and half a dozen rockers for the handsome cradle. Happy workers to serve a fertile queen! Outside, a nightingale sings in the fragrant air. The child leaps inside Mary, a fish in a silver lough. She knows it is a boy child because he lies on the right side of her womb, because her right breast is full and firm, because her right eye shines more brightly than her left. All is ordered. All is controlled. All is certain. Mary glows. She is a ripe fruit. She is Queen of England and Saviour of the True Faith.

There have been whispers that Mary is old for childbed, but the confident Queen takes no notice. No blasts or fogs menace Mary's joy. God will see her through. She will bear no deformed babe, no child of spleen, no twisted stillborn creature, but a laughing, thriving prince.

"A fish in a silver lough?" I laugh out loud. "A ripe fruit?" Good God, who wrote this rubbish?

I avoid sentimentality in all forms, but especially when it is lavished upon the products of the reproductive cycle. I have never particularly liked children, nor have I paid the slightest attention to the ticking of what they call the biological clock.

Naturally, I was concerned – even shocked – to find myself pregnant. And not because I've been a good girl. Indeed my mother is envious of my past with cause. But I couldn't accept that I – Marie Flanagan – had been so careless. Can you believe it? I actually thought that at my age, a missed pill or two couldn't make any difference.

No wonder some of the junior members of staff can be heard tittering when I lumber past. Careless is a word that has never before been associated with me, either at work or at play.

The child is a boy. Yes, I have made full use of the services of modern medicine. As I've already pointed out, I don't like surprises. I took the road North, as so many Irish women do these days, where I studied the fluttering foetus on an ultrasound screen, watching a young doctor pop in a needle to withdraw a few drops of fluid. Now that I know for certain that the child is healthy, I am determined to tackle maternity as successfully as I have work. On my own terms.

I would rather have had a girl.

It is so bizarre, this bump of mine, so out of context at the age of forty-two. But the fact is that in three short weeks I will become a single parent. Max knows nothing about the baby. I have made sure of that. I took care to sever the tenuous ties that I had with him long before my condition became apparent.

Max! Never was there a more improbable lover for a woman like myself.

He was sitting in this very kitchen plucking away on that stupid guitar of his, when I told him it was over. He stood up. He was wearing jeans and a cowboy shirt, and his boots were still upstairs in the bedroom. I remember thinking how vulnerable he looked standing there in his socks. "Can I get you a glass of milk?" he said.

Just like him really. Talk about non sequiturs.

"Listen, Max, it's been fun. But we have nothing in common. We both knew that when we started."

"I know what you're thinking. You're afraid that I'll run to fat when I get older. That I'll get a flabby belly. Most men do. It's revolting! I promise you, Marie. I will not!"

Such innocence, I thought. If only he knew about the baby, then all the fun that we'd had would blow away in the face of sour recrimination. Better to escape pleasantly and lightly . . .

"Sorry, Max," I said. Then I turned upon him a cool stare. Believe me, I haven't climbed so high up the corporate ladder without perfecting the art of the withering look.

He ignored it. "When I was a boy," he said, "I found a hedgehog with a broken leg. I made him a splint. He got better. I could . . ."

"You're still a boy," I interrupted.

Max grinned. "Come here," he said. "Come here and unbutton my shirt."

It was a difficult request to turn down.

"No," I said firmly.

"But I haven't shown you the copy of *Othello* that I bought last week for 50p," Max protested. "It's in strip cartoons. You'll love it."

He was trying to spin me into the inviting web of his trivialities, but I was too much in control of myself to be caught. In the end I had my way, and the door banged shut behind him. I haven't seen him since. That was months ago.

Max . . . I still smile when I think of him. But I did the right thing. He was just a boy.

I turn back to the ridiculous book with its pink highlights. I make it a point not to dwell in the past.

Hampton Court. Late May. The hedgerows are alive with fledgling thrushes and blackbirds. The grass is a thick carpet of buttercups and daisies. Intoxicated by the heady scent of blossom, butterflies float on the breeze. All London is ready to celebrate. The tables are laid for feasting in the streets. The bonfires wait to be lit. Only the baby prince is missing. Each morning, the Queen awakes expectantly. At nightfall, she sleeps again with a still-swollen belly.

Outside the palace, young Philip leads a procession of ageing fathers of the church. As they pray, the sunlight glints off their cloth of gold. Clouds of incense drift away in the air. From her window, Mary watches. Round and round the old men go. A silver ball nestles in Mary's hand. It is a perfect plaything, round for the future King of England. Round like Mary's belly. She sees her own reflection in the silver ball. She sees a sharp nose and a spiky chin. She sees gaunt cheeks and watery eyes without eyebrows.

Thanks be to God, I think, looking up at the mirror next to the phone on the kitchen wall. My reflection holds no nasty surprises. My skin is good. My hair is healthy. And if I wear a little make-up from time to time, it is only for fun. I take good care to look after myself. I exercise and get plenty of sleep. I eat all the right things and only a couple of the wrong ones. Yes, I don't look at all bad. That's another of the many virtues in having chosen the date of my birth so well. In this day and age, women no longer grow old the way that they used to.

Hampton Court. June. Round and round the old men march, but the lilt is gone from their step. The blossom has withered on the branch. Mary has withdrawn from the window, but she does not lie in childbed. She sits on the floor, an unqueenly thing to do. Her knees are drawn up under her chin, and her belly spills between her skinny thighs onto the floor. She sits for hours, deaf to pleas that she rise. Why will the child not come? The words are frozen in her head. Why does God not bring her child?

68

Mysterious doings are afoot. Broadsheets flutter through the window, breathing loathing of Mary and her Spanish consort. A contagion of words floats through the air, black and white devils. Evil hums through floors and walls. "The Queen is dying," Mary hears. "Dropsy," she hears. "Not a child in her belly, only death."

"No!" Mary cries. "No!" On the floor she prays frantically, her knees pressed hard under her chin. She prays until she is answered. At last, she heaves to her feet. The child waits, she realises, because God is angry. God is angry, she understands, because she has been lenient with His foes. Now, for the sake of her baby, she will be lenient no longer. Mary is not a queen and a Tudor for nothing. She staggers to the window. "Burn the heretics!" she cries out. "Burn the heretics! It is God's will. For the sake of my child, do not delay!"

Hysterical, I think. The woman was mad.

The phone on the kitchen wall rings. I answer it. I hear a couple of notes like a cheeky whistle. Then a melancholy chord. I recognise the instrument. It is a guitar. I hang up the receiver. My reflection rebukes me with its flaming red cheeks.

At least I know who pushed this damned book through my letterbox. But how has he found out?

1555. Throughout England, the fires rage, fires heaped high with heretics. Men and women, nobleman and commoner. Side by side, they are consumed. They burn like saints, these heretics, with gunpowder strapped to their armpits. They call

*out for more wood to take them to God. The sky turns black;
the smell of burning flesh is everywhere. Mary, who has a
delicate stomach, sweetens the air with rosemary and juniper.
She goes nowhere without a pomander held to her nostrils. Yet
still her child refuses to be born.*

The doorbell rings. I am under siege. Will I answer it?

"Marie!" I hear him shouting. "MARIE! If you don't
let me in, I'll huff . . . and I'll puff . . . and I'll . . ."

I think of the neighbours. I open the door. Max
charges into the hallway, his arms loaded with bags and
parcels. Over his shoulder, I can see his battered van
painted with dayglo stars.

"You lunatic!" I say.

A bag drops to the floor. Tiny pink socks spill out of
the split seam. I realise with horror that the bags and
parcels are crammed with baby things.

"It is *my* baby," I insist. "You are *not* the father."

He looks at me roguishly. He doesn't believe me. "I'm
moving in," he says. "I want to rub your back and sleep in
your bed."

"You can't, Max. It is quite impossible."

"No, it's not. You just lift the sheets and jump in.
Listen to me, Marie. You look good enough to eat."

It is Saturday morning and I am still in my bathrobe.
My hair needs to be shampooed and I have not brushed
my teeth. Something furry bounces in through the open
door. I feel a nip on my ankle, as it frisks past me into the
kitchen.

"What's that?" I squeak.

70

"Our puppy . . . His name is Ultan, which is sort of like the Welsh for 'saintly.' This family needs a saintly little doggie."

"What family?" My head is spinning.

Max bangs the door shut with his behind. "I am going to be an excellent father. I'm going to chuck out my guitar and get a job in the bank."

"There isn't a bank in Ireland that would have you."

"Hmmm . . . Maybe not. In that event, I'll be a milkman."

Why am I talking to this man?

"I've got it!" he says. "I'll run a bookstall in the Blackrock Market."

His hair has grown since I saw him last. It is thick and yellow, and it stands out about his head like a lion's mane. I see that his front teeth are crooked, a detail that I've never noticed before.

"Babies are like plants," Max says. "You give them plenty of air and water and sunlight, and then you sit back and watch them grow."

"It's not that simple," I yell.

"Yes it is . . . By the way, you don't mind if we sell the dining room table? I'm going to need plenty of space to do my yoga."

We're in the kitchen now, and already my nice, neat house is a mess. Everything has been knocked askew, and the puppy is chewing on one of my new shoes. Funnily enough, I don't care.

"You're changing, Marie, I can tell," Max says. "I see you've read the book."

71

It is sitting on the table where I left it.

"Pregnant women love to read about other pregnant women," he says.

"She wasn't pregnant."

"Terrible to be alone like that." Meditatively, Max tugs on his ear. "You can't help but feel sorry for her, even if she lived a hundred years ago."

"More than four hundred."

"What's the difference, Marie? She was a very emotional woman, just the same. Not like you. Why, you've made it your business to suppress your emotions all your life."

"That's not fair!"

"Sssh." He lays a finger on my lips. "I did say you were changing, didn't I? Do you know what's going to happen to you and me? We are going to grow together like a couple of trees."

At our ankles, Ultan begins to bark.

"Quiet, boy!" Max says. "That doggie goes berserk whenever I mention trees . . . Listen, Marie . . . There's a bit in the book that I didn't mark. I'll read it to you now."

A queen weeps in Hampton Court. Her sobs echo in a barren chamber. They have taken away the empty cradle. But Mary is not alone. Black demons swarm about her head, hobgoblins of regret and despair. For Philip has said that he must leave. Affairs of state call him to Spain. He will return, he says. Mary believes him. She is the only person in all England who does.

Max closes the book. "That fella was a real shit," he says.

"Like you?"

"Not in the least." Max opens my robe and nuzzles my bump with his head. "You're like a pod about to burst," he says. "Don't talk. I can hear her little heartbeat."

"It's a boy," I say, my fingers tugging at his lion's mane. I laugh although I'm about to cry. I'm wondering just how I'm going to explain Max to my mother.

Dublin is Full
of Married Men

"Andrew has this picture book," Sam says, talking about one of his sons. "It's called *The Zoo in You*. He is obsessed with it, the way only an eight-year-old can be. It's all about the parasites that live on people: worms and lice and fungi. You know, creepy-crawly stuff. It has the most revolting illustrations."

Sam is waiting in Rose's flat, as Rose puts on her velvet beret. A Mozart piano concerto plays in the background on the CD player that Sam has bought for her. "Red suits you," he says, sliding his arms about her waist. He has come straight from his office, and his business suit is immaculate. Rose smiles at his reflection in the mirror. Later, she will undress for him, leaving the hat for last perhaps.

"When I look at myself," Sam says, "I see how old I'm getting. The other day, I discovered that I had more grey hairs than I could count. And look at this." He fingers a little mark near his ear. "It's a liver spot. My father had dozens of them before he died."

Carpe diem, Rose thinks. She tugs at Sam's earlobe and tickles his chin. "I like the way you're always touching me," he says. "And I don't mean when we're making love . . . Karen would never touch me in front of the kids."

Rose listens as she smooths on some lip-gloss. Sam is a great talker. He talks about anything and everything, as confident men do, and frequently he talks about his wife. Rose doesn't mind. She is not uninterested in Karen, whom she knew at school.

That's the thing about Dublin: everybody knows everyone else. Rose is finding its intimacy less appealing than she remembered. At the moment she is working for an art gallery near St Stephen's Green. Her rented flat is in Percy Place, and she has fixed it up so that it's most attractive. She has stripped the walls and floorboards, painting, caulking and polishing until everything shimmers. There's almost no furniture, but the big window looks out over the canal, where the boys splash when the summer days are hot.

"I like your flat," Sam says. "I like being alone with you, listening to music. It's so peaceful here. Karen never sits still. Our house is crammed full of things: toys; football boots; knick-knacks of every description. We have the most highly cultivated garden in all Killiney. You wouldn't believe the number of trellises that I've put up for that woman. Recently she's gotten into sunflowers. She pours milk on the ground around their roots. Feeding them, she says. You should see them! The damned things are already six foot tall . . . Sometimes I'd like to tarmacadam the lot."

The concerto finishes. Rose thinks of Karen, efficiently marshalling the effects of family life. Karen was always a success with the teachers and girls alike. Rose can remember her barrelling down a muddy pitch, hockey stick poised for a resounding smash. Rose can remember her glittering collection of trophies and medals.

Rose kisses Sam with her pink tongue. She likes playing Sam's dark lady to Karen's white. Like Karen, Rose has a passion for greenery, only it is not the real thing that Rose admires. Over Sam's shoulder, a huge reproduction of *The Dream*, a painting by Henri Rousseau, dominates the wall. A naked woman reclines on a sofa in the middle of the jungle. Her name is Yadwigha, and painted foliage thrives around her: enormous spiky grasses in greens and yellows; scalloped leaves like platters; tendrils spiralling overhead. Beside her, a pair of lionesses peer out with fiery eyes. Rose loves Yadwigha on her sofa in the jungle, and Rose loves Sam. She savours the sense of occasion about each of their encounters. She adores preparing her body for him: the washing and perfuming, the painting of toenails and waxing of legs.

"Perhaps we should give dinner a miss," Sam murmurs, but Rose shakes her head. Outside in his car, Rose wonders whether they should be seen together quite so publicly. Sam, however, won't hear of discretion.

"Why should I hide you?" he demands, his chin jutting out. "Do you think I am ashamed? I respect you, Rose. Do you want me to behave like a conventional lout and keep you to myself like a dirty secret?" So Rose slides down a bit, the seat leather smooth on her bare legs. "My children would adore you," Sam says. "If only I could tell them." The car speeds down the Merrion Road. Flashing past, Rose glimpses a woman with a twin buggy, two baby faces goggle-eyed, Tweedledum and Tweedledee. That was what Rose noticed first when she came back to Ireland. The hordes of children everywhere.

In the Japanese restaurant Sam and Rose drink rice wine out of thimble-sized cups. "It's extraordinary," Sam reflects, "how I've learned more about you in a couple of months, than I've learned about Karen over twenty years." A young girl in a kimono bows as she serves them: three shrimp on each octagonal dish with a sliver of green onion, and a radish cut like a flower. "Look," Sam says. "A rose, like you." He eats the radish, petal by petal. Rose studies her reflection, minute in the pupils of his eyes. With his chopsticks, he feeds her a shrimp.

"I've tried to get Karen to cook more imaginatively," he says, "but she refuses. With Karen it's always chops and two veg. Last week I brought her some dolcelatte from the cheese shop in the Westbury Mall. She wanted to know how much it cost. I wouldn't tell her. At this stage in my life, I should be able to buy a little cheese and not worry about the price. The really wealthy Japanese eat rice that has been wrapped in gold leaf. I read about it in the magazine section of *The Sunday Times*."

Thoughtfully, Rose dips a strip of raw fish into a piquant sauce. Sam's house in Killiney is comfortable. She knows because she has looked him up in the directory, then paid a secret visit. She has seen Karen's station wagon in the curving, leafy drive. She has pictured the kids piling out, after Karen has collected them from the swimming pool, slapping their soggy bags of togs against one another. She has imagined Karen busy in her utility room, machines humming, mistress of all modern conveniences. Rose reads the novels of Proust and Flaubert. She has watched the plays of Racine in the original French. Once she copied out a love poem by Rimbaud in her elegant spidery writing, and tucked it into the breast pocket of Sam's shirt.

"I want to be fair to you, Rose," Sam murmurs. "I want to treat you honourably."

They go back to her flat where she stands naked, folding her body against the rough material of his suit, her pearly flesh excitingly vulnerable. He bites her neck, and she slaps his cheek. She knocks the lights off and flings back the curtains. They make love as the curtains billow at the open window, night noises blowing in: the wavering song of a drunk; the rumbling of a lorry; the shouting of a gang of youths.

Afterwards her gaze wanders about the room. The silk of her slip shines on the back of the chair. Yadwigha points from the jungle foliage. Sam's socks lie on the floor where he dropped them, scrunched into a disagreeable heap. She rolls away from him. Later, when he thinks that she's fallen asleep, he tiptoes out, back to his white lady. Then Rose stretches, extending her limbs in the bed for she likes sleeping alone. She dreams, splendid vivid dreams with the growling of beasts and the screech of exotic birds in her ears.

Sam meets Rose once a week, most weeks, always by arrangement. Rose is Sam's business dinner, his squash night, his drink with the lads. "She doesn't suspect a thing," Sam remarks. Rose cannot imagine how Karen can be so stupid. But Rose asks no questions, leaving Karen to her cake sales and dream auctions, her meals on wheels and her Scout leadership.

"You know, Rose," Sam admits, "you're the only woman I've ever made love to apart from Karen." He pauses, but Rose makes no equivalent boast. "Karen and I were childhood sweethearts," Sam continues. "I never dreamed I could be unfaithful. I thought I'd always want to hold her hand. And I do, really, but . . . I feel so guilty. I suppose I shouldn't talk to you about her. It's disloyal."

Rose nods. For Rose, guilt is one of Sam's attractions. Rose has studied the great carved portals of medieval cathedrals with their images of the writhing damned, and she knows that guilt has always served a purpose. Sam's guilt is proof of his better nature, his desire to be good. Besides it adds a certain frisson to their relationship, the temptation of Eve's apple.

"I often think that I should tell Karen about you," Sam says.

"No," she whispers. "Please don't."

They try the Lebanese restaurant in Dun Laoghaire, sitting thigh to thigh on the sumptuous banquette. Later, their stomachs warmed by exotic spices, they head out onto the pier in the stormy summer's night. Arms laced about one another's waists, they face the wind, warm rain pelting their faces. At the mouth of the harbour, they kiss as the sea smashes on the rocks, their clothes dripping, wet bodies tangled like wrack.

The many hours that she is not with Sam, Rose keeps to herself, avoiding the companionship offered by colleagues and clients at the gallery. Instead she drifts through the city streets of her past. She recollects her happy-go-lucky days as an arts student, before a careless marriage made her desperately unhappy, before she'd fled to the Continent. She'd been only a girl then, with idealistic ideas about what life would bring. She has learned the hard way.

Rose strolls through Stephen's Green on her way to work. It is Saturday morning, too early for there to be a crowd. Ahead of her stretch the summer gardens, as lush as if painted with a bright palette, a Vuillard or a Gauguin, vibrant colours dazzling the eye. Then the shimmering image is disturbed. It's a family in tracksuits – a man, a woman, two boys and a teenage daughter – bearing down towards the bridge. Rose recognises the woman first, the bullish confidence of the hockey pitch undiminished by the passing of years. Instinctively Rose retreats.

The man is Sam. She barely recognises him in the too small T-shirt, his belly sagging over the sloppy pants of a tracksuit. It is only his mouth that persuades her, for he is talking hard, and well she knows the movement of his lips in full flight. He is gabbling to the sullen creature who slouches at his side, a daughter with a rebellious glint in her eye. "Don't tell me what to do!" Rose hears the girl mutter. Rose shrinks back into the foliage, camouflaging herself with green. She feels embarrassed, loath to be seen, but she stares out at Sam's daughter curiously. Poor thing. The girl is an unfortunate hybrid of her parents' features. Small wonder she snarls like a wild beast, resentment simmering against the parents who have made her so ugly. Rose secretly watches them pass. The boys break into a trot, ruffians veering towards the playground, the younger wiping his runny nose on the back of his wrist. Gratefully, Rose makes her escape.

Her relief is deep when she again meets the Sam that she knows, the groomed lover who preserves his best self for her. He leaves his car outside her flat, and they walk into town. Her sandals have gold filigree straps which shine against the grey pavement. In the Greek restaurant Sam refuses the retsina. "No," he insists, "we will drink red wine tonight." They down two glasses in quick succession. He pins the rose from the table vase into her curls. A wild Greek dance throbs in the background. "Yes," Sam says, "we will get drunk tonight. A bacchanal!" They weave their arms together and drink, red wine sloshing. Their lips collide, and the wine in his mouth flows into hers.

He is staring across the table. He cannot take his eyes off her. "I have been thinking about the rest of my life," he says. "I can't go on the way we've been." He wets his lips with his tongue. There's a faint glow of perspiration on his forehead. "I have decided to leave Karen."

The waiter thumps a fresh carafe of wine onto the table. A few drops splash, staining the white cloth. "Bull's blood," the waiter leers, flashing his gold teeth before vanishing.

"I can see that you're surprised," Sam laughs. "I wanted to surprise you. I wanted to remember this moment forever." Indeed, Rose's heart is beating fast. Over Sam's shoulder Karen glares, hockey stick at the ready, prepared to defend until death her big house and wronged children. "Oh, Rose," Sam says, "to find such happiness at this stage in my life. It's a miracle! They say no man ever leaves his wife for his mistress. Not in Ireland, anyway. But here I am, living proof to the contrary."

"I never put any pressure on you, Sam," Rose says. "None whatsoever."

"Exactly," Sam agrees. "I liked that. It persuaded me in the end . . . I'll see my solicitor in the morning. Karen can keep the house and the sunflowers, so long as we can have the children regularly . . . You know, Rose, you couldn't have happened to me at a better time. A couple of years ago, the kids would have been too small, and all this would have been unthinkable."

Rose doesn't bother to listen anymore. She examines the wine in her glass. There is a trace of grease floating on the top, spreading the colours of the rainbow over the crimson liquid. It is pretty enough, but it is only grease. She puts the glass back on the table.

They walk home. Sam is holding her hand. "To think that we'll be together for the rest of our lives," he says. "Just look at the moon." Overhead, Rose sees a sliver in the sky, as yellow as cheese. She raises her hand to her forehead. "Poor pet," he says, "do you have a headache? We should have taken the car." He leaves her at her door. "Your headache will be gone in the morning."

Rose stands alone on the threshold of the flat that she has made her own. She has no headache. Inhaling deeply, she admires the interesting space perfected by her own hand. It is a lover that Rose wants, not a husband with feet of clay. After switching on the CD, she takes up her pen, writing,

> Sam,
> *Ending your marriage would ruin our lives.*
> *Please don't contact me again.*
> $\qquad\qquad\qquad\qquad$ *Rose.*

She seals the letter, smiling up at the reproduction on the wall, Yadwigha, exotic in her painted jungle. Rose will not miss Sam. After all, Dublin is full of married men.

Underwear

"You have the most beautiful skin I have ever seen," he said. He wasn't talking to me, or even to Sky, but to a sow, a pearly white pig with white skin and white bristles, whose snout he was stroking with his strong white fingers; and I was taking their photograph. I was meant to be shooting the sow, but with each click of the shutter, John expanded in my frame, and the pig with beautiful skin receded into background.

I had been hired to photograph John's pigs, imports from Denmark, destined to change the profile of Irish pig-farming forever, or so John claimed. His enthusiasms had seduced me on the telephone. His words had rushed out of the receiver, spurting into my ear: "enterprise" and "deal" and "profit". So, from the first light of dawn, I'd been capturing inventive images of gleaming contours in black and white.

To think of it. Me, a photographer of pigs! But I wasn't sorry, not after I'd caught sight of John.

He thwacked the sow across her rump, and she ambled away. I realised that my job was done, our encounter over, and that John would go his way, and I mine. But I haven't got where I am without understanding initiative.

"Let me take a few shots of you indoors," I proposed unhurriedly.

"Why not?" he agreed. The way I see it, there is no point in being put off by the glint of a man's wedding ring.

I followed him into the stylish house, a vast, low-slung bungalow with a panoramic view of hill and lake. Sky toddled after me, his slight frame stooped under my heavy gear. In the distance I could hear a woman's hum.

John's study smelled of leather. He posed for me against the wood panelling, my eye drinking in with my camera the details of his life: the Chinese porcelains, the three phones, the many photographs picturing him with the well-heeled. The tentacles of his business interests clearly embraced a good deal more than pigs.

With a steady hand I positioned his head to catch the best of the light. I was feeling lucky. I had noticed only the single snap of his wife with their teenage sons.

Later, Sky sat next to me in the jeep as I negotiated the lane. "You're like a fly in a web," he said softly, stroking the downy fluff on his chin. I looked at him askance. There's something wrong with Sky's hormones, some misfiring of nature that has frozen him forever in eternal boyhood. "Yes, you are in love with that brute."

"Whatever are you talking about?" I protested. "I never saw the man before this morning."

"I know you, Kate. You are in love with John." Sky's forehead wrinkled with the effort of sounding knowledgeable.

I laughed, dismissing him, as if I found the very idea of love preposterous, but privately I vowed to polish my reserve. Don't give anything away. That's always been my philosophy.

Damn Sky anyway. The soul of indiscretion, he never shuts up. He is always telling everyone that he wears boxer shorts, because they make him feel Bohemian. And who could respect a person like that?

Back at my place, I sent Sky packing and locked myself in the darkroom. At midnight I emerged, my head alive with images of pigs. Pigs and a man. Not a man, but a colossus. I poured myself a whisky, willing the phone to ring, and ring it did.

"About those photographs," he drawled, "we need to discuss them." I knew that it was not photographs that John had in mind.

"Now?" I inquired drolly.

"Now."

We began to kiss in the darkroom, his burly body crashing into mine. Sweeping my proofs onto the floor, he ripped off my shirt like tissue paper. Together we lay down on the floor, writhing and grunting midst the pigs.

Afterwards, when I thought about it, I decided that John

86

began pilfering my underwear on that very first night. It gave me great pleasure, imagining him with my bits and pieces, stroking my blue-green camisole and burying his face in the matching satin knickers. I wondered where he kept them, my intimate things. Perhaps in the back of a drawer in his study, ready to be touched when the need grabbed hold of him. I liked to picture his strong white fingers creeping into the silky recesses as he chaired a meeting, or talked on the phone. Or perhaps he secreted my treasures in his pillowcase, so that he might inhale my perfumes throughout the night, as his wife snored next to him.

I have always been a buyer of fine underwear, selecting only the best fabrics for wearing against my skin. Laces and silks and satins, everything perfect. A tiny stain or a minuscule tear has been enough to make me throw out the most expensive gossamer. I want things to be perfect.

Sky says that I like having my own way and that's why I'm a photographer. It's the control, he says. I know what he means. It is true. I can invent the world that I want in my pictures by searching and focusing and cropping and superimposing. Yes, my shutter captures only the reality that my own brain has selected.

And people say that the camera never lies! Of course it does!

The photographs that I'd taken for John were a huge success, arresting portraits of strange creatures, rooting and nuzzling in a moonscape of field. In fact they scarcely looked like pigs at all. Through my connections the photos were reproduced widely, and the profitability of John's enterprise was assured.

And so our encounters were enhanced by the spice of success. He always arrived in the dark hours, sometimes ringing first, more often not. I fell into the habit of listening for his heavy footfall and the thud of the knocker on the door, missing him when he did not materialise. Those late, late hours seemed destined for the primitive things that we did, hours that bristled with ever more inventive couplings.

I made a study of him, an intimate study, taking thousands of photographs in my head. They were grainy images of masculinity: thick-torsoed and taut-bellied, pictures that I could call to mind at will. I explored his pores, the folds of his groin, the whorls of his nostrils. I came to understand his body better than my own.

I never said a word to him about my vanishing underwear. But when I replaced the missing garments, I began to buy for him as much as for myself, letting my fingers stray from the whites and pastels towards the bordello purples and reds that he might fancy.

When he holds my underwear, does he see my soul for the many-coloured thing that it is? Does he understand that never before have I let a man get so close to me?

Occasionally I thought of nicking his own black Y-fronts, and the vest with the plunging neckline that frames the matted hair curling on his chest; but how could I, without breaking into that luxurious bungalow that he occupies with his wife? Surely it would be madness to risk prison for the man. Or would it?

* * *

I was aware that something strange was happening to me. It began with my leaving small jobs undone – plugs and leaky taps – little things which I have often fixed in a minute. But why did I give up the satisfaction of doing them myself? For the dubious pleasure of asking him, so I might ooh and aah over his skills! If anyone had told me a month ago that I could behave so girlishly, I would have scoffed, but not anymore.

My concentration fell by the wayside next. There I was, deep in the simplest of shoots, absorbed by the shadows and light of a waif modelling glamorous rags, when, without warning, his face reared up in front of my lens, and my work was spoiled.

Never before have I ruined a picture for any man.

But when I should have been planning new projects, I wasted hours pouring over business pages, wading through verbiage towards the golden buoy of his name. No place was sanctuary. Even in the supermarket, while selecting cherries and unblemished grapes, I'd spot him at the top of the aisle, but when I raced with my trolley to catch up, no one would be there.

The time came when I pawed through my negatives, yes *those* negatives – pigs and man, man and pigs – to hunt out the one that I needed. Holding it up to the light, I saw his shapely form revealed, confident-eyed in his leather study, arms akimbo, ready to rule the world and me. I taped the negative to my shoulder and sat in the sun until his image was burned deep into my skin.

* * *

"You've got it bad," Sky said. I no longer bothered to deny it.

Sky was sweeping the floor in my darkroom, slowly but methodically. He put the brush away into the press. He considered me thoughtfully, tapping his cheek with a droopy forefinger. "Take me, Kate," he said, "like you'd swallow a spoonful of medicine. I'd be good for you. Take me. You are in need of a cure." Sky's hand dropped towards his trousers, apparently poising to unzip.

"Why are you laughing at me?" Sky said.

"Because you are being ludicrous!"

"I am being serious!" Sky wriggled like a friendly dog. "Try me," he coaxed. "You won't be sorry. I am a very sensitive lover. We'd have loads of fun. I'd even let you get on top."

But I shook my head.

Sky perched on the edge of the stool. "Let's look at this rationally, Kate. You don't fancy me and I know that you don't. Nor do I fancy you either. But something has got to get that brute out of your heart. He is destroying you."

The man was a comedian.

"Run along home now, Sky," I said. "I'll see you next week."

"Well, if you change your mind in the meantime . . ." Amiably, Sky trotted out the door. I watched him go with relief. I could no more go to bed with Sky, than I could with a fish.

* * *

It was four o'clock in the morning. John rolled off me, dragging the bedclothes onto the floor. He strode in his skin to the bathroom, not bothering to close the door. I couldn't tear my eyes away, as he rubbed and slapped himself in the shower. The water bounced from his gleaming body into puddles on the floor.

But why was he so intent upon washing? Why did he splash himself with cologne? Why did I never see him in the daylight? Did we talk enough? Did we talk at all?

My head spun with anxiety.

He nuzzled me, grunting good-bye. The front door slammed behind him. Did he love me? Full of anxiety, I rushed to my drawers and counted. Another pair of panties, gone! I zoomed in upon the image of lavender silk, nestling in his strong hands. Then I willed his wife to discover. What then? He'd pretend they were a present for her alone. She wouldn't believe him. She couldn't believe him. They were ever so dainty, too flimsy for a porcine frame like her own.

Yes, I had all the pictures worked out in my head: a sequence of rage and accusations, the end of a marriage. Then I drew up short. Could I possibly be looking through a filter, a filter that blurred reality? Was my judgment askew? Was Sky right? Had John damaged me beyond recognition?

I rushed to the mirror, but the woman I saw there was a stranger. That twisted mouth? Not mine. Those weary eyes? Not mine. That splotchy complexion? Never. Not me. Dear God, the woman in the mirror looked the sort who would wear washed-out knickers, their slack elastic knotted at the waist.

In my studio I set up with care, flooding a black background with harsh light. I scoured my face to the bone. I let my hair hang in greasy clumps. Setting the automatic timer on my Nikon, I posed. With each click of the shutter, I rotated my head infinitesimally, so as to leave no part of my misery unexposed.

They floated up out of the developing trays, the 8 by 10 enlargements, haggard and horrible images of myself. I clipped them on the wall to dry.

Maybe it is true what they say, and the camera doesn't lie after all.

Sky stared at my pictures, shifting from foot to foot. His baby face was shocked. "These are ghastly," he said. "You are perverting your talent." With gentle fingers he removed the photographs from the wall. He held them over the bin. "I should burn them," he said. He hesitated, glancing at me, as if he expected me to interfere.

The old Kate would have yelled with outrage at his presumption. But the new Kate held her tongue.

He could do what he liked with my things.

"On second thoughts, I'd better file them," Sky said, slipping my self-portraits into a folder.

Sky cleared a frog from his throat. "I've something to tell you, Kate. I've lied to you. I said that I didn't fancy you. The fact is that I love you."

Disbelieving, I turned towards him, hoping against

hope that I'd misheard. I hadn't. There in his features I saw it all, my own image, the seaminess of a secret passion, the stain of my obsession. I looked away, revolted.

"I know," he said. "Don't say a word. I apologise. It's embarrassing, but I had to tell you anyway. And there's something more. Look."

In his boyish hands he held out my underwear, the satin briefs, the blue-green camisole, all my precious bits and pieces. A scrap of lavender silk fluttered from the pocket of his jeans to the floor.

"Not you," I shuddered. "No, no, no, anybody but you." I laughed until I began to cry. I flailed him with my fists. He bore my blows patiently until I pushed him away like a feather.

"Wait!" he cried. "Don't be too hasty. I'd mind the children and do the ironing. Any woman with a bit of sense would prefer me."

"You're right," I said bitterly, "any woman with a bit of sense would." Then I turned my back on him and limped out the door.

The Chiropodist

"For better, for worse." On the day that I married
Hannah, I took the priest's words seriously, so seriously
that four years and thirty-seven days passed before I
forgot them in a moment of impetuousness. I was fifty-
three years old on the day that I married Hannah, and
she was twenty. I went into the arrangement in perfect
good faith, without intimation of the sulphurous pit that
lay ahead. But before I plunge into the smoke and stench
of that tempestuous day, let me take you back, back to
the remarkable beginnings of a wonderful romance.

Oh, the foot, the foot! Its complexities are so
commonly misunderstood. How taken for granted each
one of its twenty-six bones is, that is, until something
goes wrong!

Anyway. Believe me when I say that my snail's
progress to the altar was no slur upon my masculinity. *Au
contraire*, I was always in complete possession of the
appropriate quantities of testosterone, and the hairs on

94

my body sprouted in full profusion at the normal locations, with particular abundance on my scalp. But before I met Hannah, there'd been no reason to rock my boat. For I was one of the fortunate few who had found complete happiness in work. Hannah opened my eyes to other possibilities. Yes, Hannah made me aware that there was more to life than attending to the eruptions and malformations that presented in my clinic.

My dear, dearest Hannah. How that young woman changed my life! I understand that there are gossips who found the December-May aspect of our relationship comical; not to mention other begrudgers who sneered because our marriage was celebrated before the grass had grown upon Mother's grave. As if I were a drowning man grasping at a straw! You and I know this to be nonsense. You and I know that the truth is simple: that I married because I fell in love. To be precise, I fell in love with Hannah's feet, then worked my way up from there.

The child arrived at my clinic one rainy afternoon with a minor complaint. Not that it was minor to her. Her face was white with pain. *Pauvre enfant!* She just couldn't tolerate suffering – or even inconvenience – in any way. When she limped into my rooms, real tears glowed in the corner of her eyes. At first I was unmoved. I listened with my customary indifference to the sound that I'd heard so many times before: the swish of tights being removed behind the screen. I certainly didn't expect what emerged. Her exquisite feet! So perfectly proportioned! Such pearly skin and the straightest of toes! All my years of experience and reserve crumbled in an instant. I stared helplessly, bewitched, unable to accept that these models of perfection might be flawed in any way. She rescued me – sweet stranger – by leading my melting fingers to the tiniest of corns on her dainty baby toes. As in a dream, I heard myself suck in my breath, then with one deft stroke, I turned the horny offender into a memory. She sighed with pleasure.

Hers was a languid little sigh that lingered in my ears. I became acutely conscious of my telltale reactions – the stirrings of mind and body that measured the enormity of my feelings. How astonished I was! For in the past, only the abnormal foot had thoroughly engaged my enthusiasms and exercised my ingenuity. Now my faculties were aroused completely, and all for feet devoid of ills to succour or soothe!

"You have the hand of God," she said softly. "My tears have quite evaporated."

The tears! Her tears that I had so callously ignored. *Mea culpa!*

But still I could not look up. I could not tear my eyes away from her sole, which yet nestled in my palm. So loath was I to abandon its bald smoothness that I invented unnecessary tasks, probing the moist dark recesses between her toes, letting my hands creep up the creamy flesh towards the ankle bone, where I sought her pulse. Pressing the palps of my fingers against that pristine skin, I measured the rhythmic pulses of her heartbeat, as if my life too depended upon them. To my surprise, my questing fingers detected an increase in pace. Could it be? Was it possible that her heart too was quickening at our proximity? Impulsively, my hands ran up her calves, where they began to massage, ever so tenderly.

She sighed again, more fully, more expectantly, and then! more demandingly! forcing me to look up. She was looking directly at me! How they dazzled me, those eyes, her eager eyes.

"You know how to take the pain away," she murmured. "Yes, in this difficult brutal world of ours, you understand how to make a girl feel good."

Her words made me shudder with delight. For it was true. It pleased me to serve. Accustomed to caring for women, I was thrilled that Hannah had recognised this in me. I felt at once the clarity of the understanding between us, smashing down the barrier of years. As I had examined her foot, she had looked into my soul. And what more could love be than such a frank exchange? Yes, from that moment in time, I was prepared to look after Hannah forever. In no way would I stint.

"*Je t'aime*," I said to Hannah. I was in love. And like any honourable man in love, I proposed marriage, then and there. Fortunately, as luck – and my profession – would have it, I was already on bended knee.

I have always been grateful for Mother's rearing me to be a gentleman. From my first wobbling steps, she immersed me in the requisite attitudes and manners. She taught me what was right. She saw to it that I had the necessary education and respect for authority. And she encouraged me when I decided to go into chiropody. Chiropody!

Such a noble profession! The profession *par excellence* for the gentlemanly man, demanding the utmost of intellect and compassion. The hideous conditions that I am called upon to ameliorate! The blistering effusions, warped nails and ostler's toes! People respect me the way that they would a doctor, but the joy of it is that my life remains my own. For the chiropodist there are no peremptory summonses at any hour of the day or night. From the time I began to practise, I formed the habit of scheduling appointments around the heart of the day, just so I might stroll home and prepare a meal. *Répas de deux*, that's what I called cooking for Mother, a small joke at the expense of the ballet, if you follow me. And I never cooked beans on toast either, but a gourmet meal, salmon poached with dill, or breast of chicken and apricots.

Yes, I am very fond of cooking, French *cuisine*, by inclination. A gentleman's skills must be various. I am proud to say that these very hands of mine, which are so capable when it comes to verrucas and bunions, are equally useful in the kitchen. I can bone a chicken and peel onions with the best of them. Indeed, I whipped up my own wedding cake myself, sculpting the icing into a frilly fantasy with sugar mice peeping over the edge of the top tier.

Like any ordinary man, I regarded procreation as the *raison d'être* of marriage. I wanted nothing more than a tribe of children scampering about our happy home on their tiny pink feet. But in spite of my best efforts, nothing happened. I didn't lose heart, for I felt confident that our difficulty would be resolved. If my experience was limited, my reading was not, and I deduced that the power to rectify matters might rest in my own hands. Since I was no longer young, I set about a sustained course of action to improve my potency. I wore loose trousers, took cold baths and initiated a regime of abstinence punctuated by vigorous coupling at optimum times.

Additionally, I made a thorough study of the technical art of foreplay, subscribing to the principle that an aroused female is a receptive one. What unexpected pleasures I discovered in the practise of this principle! I took her little feet into my hands and I kissed them. I sucked each toe in turn, letting my tongue play along the delicious nail grooves, as I contemplated the little angels that we would engender. Inch by inch, I feathered my way up into her body until she was ready to dissolve in a sea of satisfaction.

In fact I pleasured her so thoroughly that, one evening, she fainted. Yes, without warning, at the very height of intimacy, Hannah went limp and slithered right out of the bed onto the floor. Were it not for my presence of mind, she would have banged her head. Poor Hannah! She looked so helpless, stretched out naked and insensible on the floor. I fanned her frantically. She groaned. I rubbed her wrists, their slender veins looking too blue against the alabaster of her skin. At last, thankfully, her eyelids fluttered open.

"Dearest Albert," she whispered, "have I frightened you?"

Mutely, I shook my head, but my heart was thudding.

Her eyes latched onto mine. With a tentative finger, she stroked the floorboards upon which she lay. "Life is so hard," she said. "Desperately hard. And I am so terribly tired."

Guiltily, I propped her head upon a pillow and covered her girlish body with a quilt. I blamed my acrobatics for her loss of consciousness. However, in the very act of making her comfortable, a thought wormed into my mind: that the root of our infertility might be lurking inside her young bones.

I banished the idea at once, but from that moment on, I believe that I eyed my wife differently. I started to notice her tiny frailties, a lingering cough here, a touch of breathlessness there. Concerned, I suggested that she quit her job in the children's nursery. "To make conception more probable," I argued plausibly, grateful for her ready consent. I began bringing her breakfast in bed, determined to give her every creature comfort that she deserved. And the first time that I saw her stagger beneath the weight of a basket of washing, I took to hanging the clothes out on the line myself.

It was no trouble to me really. I'd always helped Mother around the house, and managed perfectly well after Mother was gone. I wasn't afraid of scrubbing a few floors. Besides, Hannah's smile was reward in itself. "You're too good to me," she'd say, and then laugh in her charming musical way.

But no matter how much housework I did, nothing seemed to staunch the flow of my darling's decline. Bit by bit, her gait grew more uncertain. The tears welled in my eyes, as I watched her pitiful struggle from kitchen to dining room, clutching at the walls to support herself.

I bought her a walking stick. "Albert," she smiled, "you are the best man that a woman could want. If only these naughty feet of mine would bear my weight reliably."

I took them in my hand – her exquisite feet – and marvelled that Fate could play so cruel a trick. How I longed to heal them! To paint them with therapeutic tincture! To strengthen them with poultice or ointment! But so long as they betrayed no tangible mark of their disorder, what corrective procedure could a conscientious practitioner undertake? How frustrated I was! Yet I confess: part of me rejoiced that the little feet remained unmarked. How much worse it would have been if her growing disability had caused them to twist or contort, to become mere grotesque appendages.

I encouraged my darling to pass more hours in bed. I collected books and chocolates and armfuls of flowers to console her. I took on the shopping and the ironing and the washing-up; in short, I became responsible for all the little domestic tasks that need doing in a happy home. Eventually, when she could barely stand unaided, I purchased a wheelchair, and helped her to totter the few steps from bed to chair, where I tucked a lap rug around her knees to prevent her taking a chill.

I continued to take particular care of her feet, scooping

out the debris from under the nails, the toe-jam as we'd called it in boarding school. I buffed and massaged, stimulating her circulation to compensate for her stationary life. But as affectionate as my attentions remained, my hands strayed no more towards the regions closer to her heart. Somehow, it no longer seemed appropriate.

She didn't seem to mind.

I was often fatigued between the demands of my practise and caring for Hannah, but I never complained. I genuinely felt no inclination to protest. My poor little Hannah, *mon pauvre enfant*! How I pitied her, revolving between bed and wheelchair, and wheelchair and bed!

If only I'd been a bad man instead of a good man! If only I'd been less of a gentleman, the tragedy need never have occurred!

For I want you to know (on the understanding that you won't tell) that my beloved became something of a tyrant. "There's dust on those books," she'd shout. And I'd dust as if my life depended upon it.

"And look at the state of those floorboards! A blind man would know they need waxing!" So I'd buy wax and apply myself until my knees and shoulders ached, while she'd tap that floor with her walking stick, urging me always towards more efficient endeavours. I accepted her instructions as though they were the word of God. You see, I recognised how much she enjoyed acting my superior, and I encouraged it. Why begrudge small pleasures, where so many of the normal satisfactions were denied?

I should have abused her! I might so easily have found other feet to console myself with. Why didn't I? When I think of it! I should have used my clinic as a cover for the most systematic carry-on! All those helpless women, you know, feet bared, queuing up for comfort. The services that I might have provided! If only I had, then the steam that ultimately exploded would surely have dissipated in the wind, long before that terrible morning arrived.

It began like any other morning. I helped Hannah into the bath. I sat in the steam, reading out loud to her.

Dear God! I remember it as if it were yesterday! The smell of the bath oil, and me drying the nape of her sweet neck, patting gently with a fluffy towel. That alabaster skin! I selected a lace nightgown that didn't disguise the girlish contours of her body. I kissed her good-bye, then left for work. But by the time that I arrived at my clinic, what had been a grumbling in my stomach had become a persistent ache; so I decided to cancel my appointments and return home for the day.

I heard the music as I turned my key in the door. The galloping strains of *Petrouchka*! I smiled, pleased that Hannah should be listening to fine music. I even paused in the hallway for a moment, letting the ravishing cadences wash over me. Already I was feeling better.

Then I noticed her wheelchair. It was empty. My heart quickened. Swiftly I flung open the door to the sitting-room. The music was loud, so loud that she didn't hear me. But I believe that she wouldn't have heard me anyway, for she was lost, quite lost, in her . . . yes, in her dance! Oh, the treachery of her duplicity! Hair floating through air, she leaped from the table in a dazzling display of sure-footedness. Lithe as a cat, she skimmed across the floor – those very floorboards made to gleam by my own hands! The frothy nightgown fluttered over her fluid limbs, as she kicked and gambolled. Unseen, I watched her eyes, misted with a bliss that had nothing to do with me.

I clubbed her to death. No! That's untrue; I've told you a lie, for which I apologise. The case has been stated too dramatically. The very words – "clubbed her to death" – imply a brutality of the most grotesque nature, a brutality of which a gentlemanly man is incapable.

In fact I only hit her once, one deft stroke to the back of the head which dropped her like a stone. Dearest Hannah! She never knew that I'd found her out. Thanks to me, she remained safe in her fantasy world until the end. In court, I listened with some satisfaction as an expert explained how that single blow had pushed her brain into the bottom of her skull.

I used the footrest off her wheelchair.

There was almost no blood, not from the death wound anyway. Ever so gently, I turned her onto her back so that I might attend to her feet. She looked much as usual, with only the slightest trickle drizzling from her nose.

I went about my business methodically. *Quels pieds jolis!* I can picture them still, exactly as they were, those

104

exquisite feet that changed my life. Yes, I did everything that it was possible to do to those feet, short of amputation. In court, they spent two hours detailing the extensive injuries, circulating a dozen photographs. They even displayed ten glass jars, each one containing a perfect toenail suspended in preservative, the ten toenails that I had excised that day with my customary precision. "Premeditated," they said, again and again, punctuating every piece of evidence with that gloomy word. "Premeditated."

To tell you the truth, they said some very nasty things about me indeed.

I neither challenged the prosecution's case, nor hinted at mitigating circumstances. It would have been churlish to tell them the real story, a story that necessarily would have cast my Hannah in a disagreeable light. No, they heard nothing from me about the liar and cheat that she was.

Mon Dieu! I weep great tears when I think about it. And I had always imagined that Mother would have liked her!

In retrospect I realise how poorly Hannah and I understood one another. What a strange thing human relationships are! How very peculiar the ordinary man finds them!

I got life. Yes, the jury convicted me, and the judge gave me life.

How fortunate that Mother didn't live to see my cell. It would have distressed her. Her only son! But all is fair. I don't mind. No gentleman grudges paying the price.

I miss my clinic. But happily, my memory is good, and I can bring it all to mind, all the other less exquisite feet with which I might have fallen in love. So many possibilities that might have led elsewhere! Sublime speculation! Believe me, it is a most absorbing pastime.

Lift Me Up and
Pour Me Out

I: *Butcher*

Jane. Little Jane. Blondy hair, pink skin, the size of a button. The tiniest of Mummy's babies. Mummy had great big strapping babies. Nine pounds, ten pounds, eleven pounds. Great monstrous rubbery ugly babies. Then me. Five pounds nothing and pretty as a dolly.

They dress me up in pink and white. They buy me pretty shoes. Itsy bitsy black patent leather shoes, shiny as glass. Daddy lifts me like a feather, high up onto the table, and I dance. Tiny ballerina, spinning round and round. Everybody smiles and claps. Pretty little Jane. First I bow, then I sing. "I'm a little teapot, short and stout . . ."

I wouldn't cry. Never. Not if I fell and banged my knee. Not little Jane. Not like the monster babies who howled the house down. That's what my Daddy says they did, anyway.

107

Daddy sleeps in the big bed with Mummy. His shirts are in the wardrobe. His bottles are in the cupboard. Rows of soldiers, left-right! Green glass, ruby glass. Mummy's nightie is lacy white. She floats into the bed like a butterfly. In the mornings, there's a funny smell.

Mummy plays the piano. Up and down, down and up, fingers flying over the keyboard. Ssh! We mustn't talk, not when Mummy's playing piano.

In our family we're not allowed to play in the road. Mummy says it's vulgar. So we play indoors. And the big ones fight on the stairs. Not me. I wouldn't fight. Never. I'm too good.

The boys sleep in one room, the girls in the other. The girls have a comforter with roses and a brown spot where the iron burnt it. The boys have a woolly blanket that scratches. Under the beds there are dollies hiding. And trains, a tea set and a toy circus.

Under our house the butcher keeps his shop. He thumps upstairs in his big black boots. Boom, boom! His head is big and curly, and there's hair all over his chinny-chin-chin. There's blood on his butcher apron. There's rent money in the pocket of his butcher trousers. He counts it out into Daddy's hand. One, two, three, four . . . A shiny copper spins towards my shiny shoe. I pick it up quick and they laugh.

Mummy is playing the piano. The rings on her fingers twinkle like stars. Daddy taps his toe and drains his glass.

The butcher's shop is white in the mornings. Whitey floor, whitey counter, whitey walls. A lorry rumbles up

108

and stops. The butcher lifts the leg of a cow onto his back. In he stumbles, in his big black boots. By dinnertime everything's red. There's meat everywhere. Slabs and lumps, and a basin of blood. The butcher keeps a saw just for bones. When he's done, there's a heap of sticky sawdust on the floor.

The room behind his shop is cold. There are big hooks in the walls, and two halves of a pig's head, split like an apple. The piggy eyes are missing. Upstairs, I can hear the piano.

The butcher lifts me like a feather, high up onto his wooden block. I dance. Tiny ballerina, spinning round and round. I bow, then I sing. "I'm a little teapot, short and stout . . ." But the butcher shakes his big head. Ssh, he says. He puts a finger on his lips. The butcher has a gold tooth. There are holes under the hairs of his beard. His eyes shine like burning coals.

No! His hairy mouth is on top of mine. His big tongue chokes me. Stop! I can't breathe. His hand inside my legs is ice. Stop!

I run up the stairs, up, up! The butcher's laugh runs after me. Mummy is playing the piano. "Hold me Mummy!" I shout. "I'm cold! Like ice! Let me sit on your knee."

"Later," she says, shaking her head.

"Please!"

"Can't you see? I'm practising." Her fingers fly. Up and down. Down and up. Her lovely hair drifts over her eyes.

Colder than cold, I lie on the floor, ear down, teeth rattling. I can hear the butcher in his big black boots.

Boom, boom! I know why he wears those boots. It's because he has no proper feet at all. Only hoofs like a cow, trotters like a pig. His big, big tail curls under his bum to wriggle down his trouser leg. Even with closed eyes, I can see it twitch.

Mummy has made me a new jumper. There's a princess on the jumper with a golden crown. I hate the princess. I hate the crown. Mummy pulls the jumper over my head. It's too tight. Too tight! I scream and scream, but I don't cry. Never. I throw the jumper on the floor.

"Bold girl!" Mummy says.

But I'm good, I shout, only nothing comes out. I want to sit on her knee. I want to be cuddled. I want to curl up inside her and stay there forever.

"What's come over you?" Mummy says. "Such a pretty new jumper. And it's too small for your sisters, too." She pulls the jumper over my head, then marches away to the piano.

The big black boots thump up the stairs. There's rent money in the butcher's trousers. He counts it out into Daddy's hand. One, two . . .

There's a princess on my jumper with a golden crown.

"Pretty little thing," the butcher smiles. His heavy paw reaches out. His gold tooth gleams. His tongue is red like blood. He laughs. He counts the money out into Daddy's hand.

I sit in the corner, cold and quiet. Only the princess burns on my front, black from the butcher's touch, black like my lips from his mouth, black like my insides from his horrible hand.

Daddy's pockets are heavy with bottles. Clinkety-clink. He lines them up in the cupboard. Rows of soldiers, left-right. Green glass, ruby glass.

I steal the scissors from the kitchen drawer. I cut off the princess's head. I tear the threads from her neck and unravel her crown. I scream and scream, only nobody hears. The others are fighting on the stairs, but the devil lives below. I don't know why my Daddy lets him. Mummy is playing the piano.

II: *Spanish Boys*

My God. How I long for the hot summer sun and the nailing shut of the school door. The fact is that I intend to become a woman as soon as summer arrives. But not a woman like her. Sexless freak.

Mum. Sometimes I picture her drifting through a grassy field in a flowing white gown. Free of sweat or stain. And what does she discover at the bottom of the field, only a grand piano? So, down she sits at this piano to tinkle out – guess what – the same old tune, that horrible Faust waltz that she's been playing ever since I can remember. End of fantasy.

Mum just makes me want to scream with laughter.

Mum always imagined that I'd play the piano too. The piano teacher came to our house once a week for years. The old goat carried a stick for jabbing at the correct keys, whenever I played the wrong ones, and she suffered from an excess of facial hair. Naturally I refused to practise. "You'd better practise, Jane," Mum said. "You'd want to make something of yourself."

111

"Why should I practise?" I answered back.

Does the woman think I'm a dodo? Anyone can see that practise hasn't done a thing for her. Who'd want to end up like Mum, sitting at the ivories, day in, day out, hammering out the one loony tune until it gives everyone the creeps?

My spots disgust her. "Fruit," she says, averting her eyes. "You should eat more fruit and vegetables, Jane." So off I trot to the kitchen, where I eat. Everything except fruit and vegetables. I mix flour with water into a rubbery goo and wad it into my mouth. I spoon butter out of the dish. I scrape fat from the grill pan. Then I scoff a jar of jam and a jar of pickles. I'd eat the glass if I could. If it moves, I'll eat it. If it's dead, I'll eat it. If it wriggles like an eel, I'll swallow it whole. Watch me!

Sometimes I eat so much that I puke it right up, but – not to worry! – after a few minutes, I can start all over again. There is no end to the room inside me. My tummy can stretch like a balloon. The sweet shop is right around the corner. I am wild for circus toffees. Two for a penny, four for tuppence, twelve for sixpence, and twenty-four the shilling. I steal the money from Mum's purse. She doesn't notice. The silver wrappers flutter round my ankles.

Mum is a teetotaller, but Dad takes a drink. So would I, if I were married to Mum. Yes, Daddy understands how to have a good time, and I'm a chip off the old block. In our house we have been known to run out of bread or milk, but never out of bottles. Rows of soldiers, that's what I call them. Dad carries a silver flask inside the breast pocket of his coat. Mum looks the other way when Dad takes a swig.

Our house is impressive from the outside. It's big and boxy with a red brick façade. But the insides have never been finished properly. Rooms are uncarpeted, cupboards are half built. Ever since I can remember, a new bath has waited in the dining-room like a white queen, only there aren't any taps. And they're all gone now, my brothers and sisters, the boys mostly to England, Katy to a flat in town, Clare dead in a car crash. Yes, they're all gone except for Sharon and me, and we don't speak to one another, not unless we have to. We flit through these rooms like ghosts, the tinkle-tinkle of the Faust waltz always in our ears.

I slip off my clothes and look in the mirror. Really look, taking my time, opening my legs like a scissors, fingering the hard-to-see folds. To think of all the fuss that's made over what is nothing more than a few square inches of anatomy, common to more than fifty per cent of the population. Mum goes on and on about it, shaking her head and whispering how girls have to be particular. The nuns at school are even worse. They pretend it doesn't exist.

My God. I love saying those two words. My. God. "Thou shalt not take the name of the Lord thy God in vain," Mum says. Well, that's what you'd expect her to say, wouldn't you?

"But Mum," I explain, like I was talking to a baby, "I

do not take His name in vain. I am merely communicating with Him. One to one. Speaking to Him. *You* would call it praying. I call it marking out my territory, like a tiger sprays his in the zoo. Why shouldn't He belong to me as much as to anybody else?"

"You were such a lovely child, Jane," my Mum says, a sour look on her puss. Whatever my views on Mum, I get the feeling they're reciprocated. Definitely.

In general, I enjoy elaborating upon my many unusual theories. Especially to the nuns. I love the shocked look on their faces when I say something daring. I don't mind the lines they dole out. Fifty lines here. A hundred lines there. So what? Nobody makes me cry. I never cry. Not Jane. Never. Not even if the nuns gave me one million lines, my thoughts wouldn't change, not one little bit.

I believe that Mum should have been a nun herself instead of giving birth to the tribe of us. I've tried to imagine her in the sack with Dad. All I can picture is the look of disapproval on her face as she calculates how high she must lift her nightie, white of course, to make herself available to him. No wonder Dad's got himself a woman. Mistress is the word. I've seen her lipstick on his handkerchief. It's a purplish-pink colour, that lipstick, much too vigorous for a dried up stick like Mum.

My God. The long days parch the grass at last, and they strut through our lanes: Spanish boys, army from the South. Their eyes are black, their hair is slicked over dark foreheads. How I love the strangeness of their language. It fills my head like drink, whirling me away from the ordinary things that bore me stiff. Spanish boys. For them, I can bend and sway like a willow. There is henna in my hair and mascara on my lashes. My fingernails grow into oval moons.

Pedro, Juan. I play them one against the other, wriggling fish on lines. We drink cider in the field. We watch the orange sun dropping down. I kiss you, Alfonso, Carlos. I kiss you, Miguel. Your mouths are soft and wet and warm. Your bodies are hard. Your names are as beautiful as stars. I wouldn't look twice at an Irish boy, not after you.

III: *Bride*

Daddy's finger has gone all crooked, as if there's a bent piece of wire stuck inside. Mum says that it serves him right. Daddy has gone into hospital to get the finger straightened. They have it strapped tight between two splints, but they still won't let him out because he has an awful pain in his stomach. The doctor says it's an ulcer. Poor old Daddy. He's not meant to drink on the ward, only most nights I sneak in a bottle of laced Lucozade, because I don't like the thought of hospital at all. Horrid old hospital with its pea-green corridors, and the lights that make people look like strays from *The Night of the Living Dead*. And the ghastly items one sees. Those metallic kidney-shaped basins with unspeakable objects floating in them. Yuck. No, my Daddy wasn't meant for a hole like this.

"Jane," he says, waking up to the sight of me and the

Lucozade. "Sometimes I think you're the only person in this world who understands, really understands me."

"Course I am, Daddy." I give his pale cheek a pat. It's true, what he says. We're the best of pals, Daddy and me. The fact is, I know secrets about Daddy that nobody else knows, but I keep my mouth shut. In turn, I am the apple of his eye, and he always puts in the good word for me, whenever I need it.

I pour the booze out from the Lucozade bottle into Daddy's water glass, take a swig myself, then watch him drink. His hand shakes and the whites of his eyes look yellowish. But the booze soon brings a glow to his cheeks, thanks be to God. I perch on the bed, holding his injured hand – on account of the glass being in the good one – and I tell him my news.

"I'm in love," I say. "Teddy – his name is Edward, only I call him Teddy – is a very superior sort of person. He doesn't look a bit Irish, even though he's from Drimnagh. And d'you know what he works at? He is a singer."

"You mean he's a pop star?"

"Really, Daddy. Didn't I say he was a superior sort of person? My Teddy sings at weddings and at funerals."

"At funerals? For Chrissake, why would anyone want to sing at a funeral?" Suddenly Daddy yanks his injured hand away from mine. He's looking as cross as a wet cat. "So what you're telling me, Jane, is that this Edward has no money?"

"Daddy," I say, a bit exasperated. "How would I know how much money the man has?"

The conversation isn't going the way I'd intended. I'd

expected the usual roguish grin and perhaps a slap on the rump. God knows, Daddy's always enjoyed hearing about the men in my life before.

"What age is he?" Daddy demands.

"He's really mature," I purr. "You know what they say about girls marrying men like their fathers?"

But Daddy doesn't seem to like this answer much either.

"Would you listen to me, Daddy?" I say. "My Teddy is lovely. He's dark and cuddly, and I feel safe when I'm with him. As if nothing could go wrong."

Daddy sniffs. "I suppose he still lives with his mother?"

"He's not queer, if that's what you're saying!"

"Don't get so huffy!" With a little grunt, Daddy sits right up in the bed. "I know you, Jane. No way are you ready to settle down. In no time at all, you'll be on to your next thrill, romantic or otherwise. By which I mean to say, you're going to wake up in the morning and see this Edward for the toad that he is."

"Toad!" I squawk.

"Yeah, toad. Warts and all." Then Daddy gives me the wink before dropping back onto his pillows. And, although I'm annoyed, I don't say a word, only I wink in return, because part of me is awfully glad to see that he's not too sick to be cheeky.

Daddy doesn't look like himself on those pillows. Those pillows make him look a lot older than Teddy, although there's really only the couple of years between them. There's a photograph of Daddy that I always carry in my handbag. In that photo he is posed like a politician

117

outside the Shelbourne Hotel, hands on his hips, a rakish grin on his face. His suit is gorgeous and his dark hair rumpled. He is not unlike Teddy in that photograph. Only Daddy never sings except when he's very drunk. Which, come to think of it, is often enough.

I take my father's hand again. I don't give up easily. I have to get Daddy to like Teddy now. The two most important men in my life have got to be friends.

"Teddy . . ." I begin.

"Not tonight, Jane," Daddy frowns. "Don't waste precious time talking about your latest Romeo tonight."

But the wheels in my head are whirring fast. I can be enterprising when I put my mind to it. It won't be the first time that I've twisted my father around my little finger.

"For Chrissake, I wish that I were shut of this place!" Daddy snarls suddenly. I jump with surprise. Bad temper is nearly unknown in my father. I see that his glass is empty.

"Same again?" I ask. He nods. "Sorry, I've no ice," I joke, but he trembles even as I pour. I can't bear seeing Daddy like this. I can't wait until he's better. Perhaps I should sweet-talk the doctor to see if he'll speed up my father's recovery.

"You'll be out of here in no time," I say. "They'll fix you up right as rain, and we'll go to the races together. I'll wear my leather mini, and people will think I'm your girl, not your daughter."

Daddy stares at the ceiling. If he's taken in what I've said, he's not giving me the satisfaction of it. "When a

118

man is trapped in a bed," he says, "his whole life unreels like an old film, spool after spool in black and white."

"Whatever are you talking about, your life's in colour," I quip. To tell the truth, I'm not all that interested in Daddy's past.

"Black and white. You're old enough to hear me out. You're a woman, aren't you?"

"You bet," I say in my sexiest voice. I concentrate hard, willing my father to laugh. More than anything, I need to hear the infectious excitement of his wonderful laugh.

"The fact is, Jane," my father says, "I've failed. Failed your mother and you and your brothers and sisters."

"Daddy, please! Would you stop being so morbid!" I try to fill his glass again, but he pushes my hand away.

"Things might have been different. There was a time in our lives when I had a knack. When whatever I touched turned to gold. Jane? Do you remember when we moved? From that place on top of the butcher's?"

"No," I say. But I shiver, although the hospital air is warmer than warm.

"Sure, why would you remember? You were only a tot when we moved. But, believe me, leaving Crumlin for the new house was the high point of my life. At last I was giving your mother what she wanted. Only right after that, everything went smash, as quickly as if . . ." My father's voice wobbles, then stops. Incredibly, I see what appear to be two fat tears dribbling down his cheeks.

I don't believe it. I don't know where to look or what to do, only at all costs I must find something to distract us both. "The Morris Oxford," I say finally. "God, Daddy, don't you remember it? The gleaming wood, the cream panelling, the shiny chrome?"

The silence hangs between us. An orderly wheels a trolley past in the corridor. It squeaks. I close my eyes. I pray in so far as I am capable of praying. Outside the window, a bin lorry is mashing quantities of hospital rubbish.

"Beep-beep!" I hear. "Beep-beep!" I open my eyes to discover Daddy honking his nose like it was the horn of a car. "Beep-beep!" A smile flickers on his lips. Thank you, God, I sing to myself. My father is smiling again, and everything is going to be all right.

"Did you think your old man could forget that Morris Oxford?" Daddy roars. "No way! By Christ, that was a motor-car made for a film star. Remember?"

I see it all, as if it were happening again. The big car pulling up to the curb. Daddy, hat cocked on the back of his head, holding the door for my mother. She slides in onto the leather. Her slim dress is linen of the coolest blue, and silk scarves flutter around her. Images of musical instruments are worked into the silk, the most perfect miniature pianos.

Then the picture melts away, leaving only my mother in her lovely blue. I really liked her that day, worshipped her, even. The memory startles. What a surprise to find such a thing, rustling in the back of my head like a dry leaf.

The next night I fly down the hospital corridor, enjoying the important tap-tap-tapping of my high-heeled boots upon the floor. When I swing round the corner into Daddy's room, there's already a delegation assembled. Mum, Sharon and Katy are all lined up in a row of chairs against the wall, po-faced like they were about to partake of the Last Supper. Pity that the rest of my siblings have emigrated, or else they'd be here too, adding their own long faces to the spooks gallery. Why-oh-why do the ridiculous members of my family find it necessary to act the misery guts-es for poor Daddy's benefit, when all he really wants is happy faces?

Anyway. I don't mind their being here – not tonight – because, as it happens, I have my morsel of sweet news. And am I ever perfumed and dressed for the occasion! I whirl round in my fluffy white fun fur, ruffling Sharon's feathers in the process, then plump myself on the edge of Daddy's bed, scorning the empty chair next to Mum. The jewel flashes with authority on my finger. "I am going to be married," I say. There's great spark in my words. I hug myself with delight, sneaking a gratifying look at the green faces of Sharon and Katy. After all, they're both older than I am, and naturally fear the shrivelling destiny of old maidenhood, which as far as I'm concerned will be their just deserts.

Mum is the first to open her mouth. "You don't think that he should have asked your father first?" she whines.

"My God, Mum," I say. "How old-fashioned can you get? That isn't the way it works any more, you know perfectly well. Besides, my Teddy isn't exactly a

121

schoolboy. You wouldn't want to make the man look ridiculous would you?"

My father is examining the diamond closely. "It's not as big as the diamond that I bought for your mother," he says.

"Just like a man," I reply. "Always worrying that size matters."

Sharon titters.

"Jane," Mum says, "you shouldn't talk like that, it's vulgar."

I look to my Dad, but if I hope to see him laughing, I'm disappointed. However, tonight, nothing but nothing is going to spoil my good humour, not even the dark thought that Daddy won't be himself again, as least not until they've sorted out his ulcer.

In the pub Teddy sits me up on the bar stool and orders champagne. I stroke the spiky hairs of his moustache, and he gives me a kiss. We are celebrating our engagement. There's a crowd with us, his friends mostly, an artsy-fartsy bunch who talk fast about books, the latest plays, and I don't know what else. It's all madly exciting. Teddy has an old-fashioned watch in the pocket of his waistcoat and a paisley cravat round his neck. His jacket is the greenest velvet. From way across the room, he looks me in the eye and begins to sing, there and then, something gorgeously soppy. At least it sounds soppy, only it's in Italian, and I don't understand a word. Teddy's eyebrows are fantastically bushy, and as black as the night. I wonder if he dyes them. When the song is finished, everyone in the pub applauds us. The champagne tickles my throat. I am bursting with happiness.

The next night, I get a surprise when I trot into Daddy's room. There's a stranger woman perched on the edge of his hospital bed. In my place, if you please, and she's gassing away like she's known him for years. And Mum is sitting straight-backed in her chair, a disapproving look on her puss, only her ear is cocked attentively. I don't know what to make of the stranger woman, who's not much to look at, being plump and oldish, and wearing a ghastly floral-print dress with shoulder pads. Then the penny drops when I recognise the colour of your woman's lipstick, a purplish-pink that I've seen dozens of times on Daddy's handkerchief. To tell the truth, I'm a bit shocked that Daddy's mistress – for she it must be – should be sitting in his hospital bedroom as if she was family, only before I can think what to do, the weirdest thing happens.

Daddy crooks his newly straightened finger. "Listen to me, Jane," he says. "Promise me now that you won't marry that toad Edward." I don't believe my ears. Not that he's said it in front of everyone. But before I can give out, the woman in the floral print grabs me and gives me a sweaty squeeze. "You mustn't ruin your whole life, my dear," she says. When I push her away, she picks up Daddy's hand instead, and starts showering it with kisses.

"I'd do anything for you," she says to him. "Anything at all." I look to see if Mum's going to strike the lovebirds dead with a flash of lightning, only she's taking in the

123

spectacle with a glazed expression that says it doesn't matter a damn.

I walk out then. I'm freaked. Absolutely freaked. I can't handle what I've seen at all.

We're in the little flat where Teddy and I are going to live. Teddy is showing me the bed that he's brought from his mother's house. He pats it and a puff of dust floats up. The wee particles glitter in the afternoon sun. I snuggle against Teddy's velvet, wriggling my torso, letting him know that I want to be kissed. But he doesn't kiss me. Instead he pours himself out a whisky and tells me, then and there, about this woman he knows, who has just thrown herself at him, this woman in a floral dress with shoulder pads and purplish-pink lipstick. "Of course I didn't touch her," Teddy says distastefully. "Why would I, when I have you?"

I thunder down the hospital corridor in a blue rage. I'm so angry that I'd like to throw one of those kidney-shaped basins and its unspeakable contents all over my Daddy. When I think of how I've kept his secrets. And for what? So he might scheme with his horrid woman to break my engagement? I slam into his room. "What's the matter with you, Daddy?" I shout. "Try whatever stunts you like! Nothing is going to put me off my fiancé!"

I am yelling so loud that my ears hurt. Only Daddy's not listening. He is lying flat on the bed. "I've got cancer," he says. "They've given me three weeks." I step back, horrified, not believing what I've heard.

He doesn't let me see him, right before he goes. Not my

skin-and-bone Daddy, with his hands on his hips and a rakish grin on his face. He was always so vain. Daddy. My God, I feel empty without him. Life is such a ghastly joke. When the funeral's over, I haven't a clue what to do with myself. So I get married, a couple of weeks later. Why not? What the hell, it's my birthday, and they say if you marry on your birthday, you'll never forget your anniversary. Not that I would anyway. However. I make a gorgeous young bride in my white lace dress. There is a winning smile plastered onto my lips.

"I now pronounce you man and wife," the priest says, yawning a little. I expect that he marries people every day of the week.

"You never cry," my Teddy says to me. "Never. That's why I love you."

IV: *The Forbidden Garden*

Teddy. I love saying his name. Teddy. Tugging on his eyebrows, I squash myself against the soft velvet of his jacket. I kiss him quick before he's had the chance to swallow, sucking the whisky warmed by his mouth into my own. When he sings in a creamy voice, I go wild. Tingling, aching, happy all at once. I'm glad he's so much older than me. He'll never have to put up with my crow's feet or wrinkles.

We have taken a gorgeous little flat. Bedroom, sitting-room, kitchenette. Private bath with a great geyser over the tub to heat the water. When the geyser's lit, it roars. From the sitting-room window, we can see the overgrown garden, which we're not allowed to use since it belongs to the flat downstairs. I wouldn't have minded my own house with a garden, but singers don't buy houses, that's what Teddy says. However, we have two eggcups, two plates that are patterned in nasturtiums, two matching bowls and two chairs that squeeze under the wee table in the kitchenette. Teddy has stuck up a shelf for the bottles. "Every home should have a cellar," he jokes, lining up the bottles over our heads. Rows of soldiers, left-right! We drink out of hand-blown goblets, shimmering blue, bought in Dun Laoghaire after Teddy sang a love-song into the wind at the end of the pier.

I keep a secret box. I call it my Teddy box. Inside it's chock-a-block with bits and bobs that commemorate my love for Teddy. There, in the tangle of scribbled notes and stray cuff links, is the tiny bread van, a battered dinky that he played with when he was a kid. Holding it, I dream of his little boy hands, playing little boy games. But when I hear his footsteps on the stairs, I squirrel everything away.

Teddy. My love, my life. Everything is perfect, quite perfect, except for one teensy problem. The bed. He brought it with him from his mother's house, together with some gruesome armchairs. The armchairs I can put up with, even though they're browner than dirt, but the bed should be right. It's not nearly big enough, not for the two of us. But size isn't the worst of it. No, that bed, coming from his mother's house as it does, seems to be already occupied. It's like she's sleeping between us, grey-purple hair splayed all over the pillow, her elastic support sock scratching my leg. With her in the bed, we don't really do it, not as much as we might. I want to make love every night, and why shouldn't I, when life is so exciting? But sometimes I can't even sleep in that ghastly bed. So I lie awake thinking how fantastic it would be to have buckets and buckets of money, and buy a dozen beds of our own.

Teddy doesn't earn much. Singers don't. But he puts every penny straight into my hand. "I don't handle money," he says. It makes me feel important, being in charge. With Teddy's cheques and my wages from the boutique, I'm learning to budget, but when we run out before the end of the week, there's murder. "It's best when the woman works too," Teddy says. So I don't tell him how fed up I'm getting, now that I can't blow my wages on a new dress. And wherever I am, I go on about him. Because you never know when people will need a singer. The night that he sang on the *Late Late Show*, the girls from the boutique were pea green, bless their hearts. But Teddy could sell himself better. The problem is, he thinks chasing work is crass. "I am an artist," he says. "People know where to find me when they want me." So he mooches about, day in, day out, drinking whisky and waiting for the phone to ring. I don't think he gives a damn when it doesn't.

He's always reading. Sometimes that's all I see, books spilling out of the cooker and fridge, books under the bed, books drifting through air. He's as quiet as a mouse when he's reading. In the mornings, he doesn't say a word, not that I think the man should be absorbed by trivia, only I wish he would talk when I'm going to be out all day, boring myself to death in the boutique.

But I love him anyway, silent or talking. I love those spiky eyebrows, a fine black for a man of his years. I love his soiled washing, his drained glasses, the cuttings from his fingernails. I'd like to be the shirt on his torso, the scarf around his neck. I'd like to curl up inside his pocket and stay there forever.

In the evenings I meet him at the pub. He sits me up, up on a bar stool, and shows me off. His friends are an artsy-fartsy crowd who talk a lot, admire my gear and buy me drinks. I toss my head back and laugh, that thrilling throaty laugh just like my father's. They bet me a fiver that I couldn't drink a bottle of whisky. "Who's buying the whisky?" I said. I can drink whisky, I can drink gin. I can drink that thick yellow stuff that looks like egg yolks. It's magic that yellow. And the more that I drink, the more that I love . . .

Teddy?

To tell the truth, it's rare that I bother to think about things. Only on the occasional morning that bumps off to a bad start – when I ladder my tights or discover an oozing spot on my chin – only then do I stop to consider our life together. In the chill of the morning the birds sing, the light shimmers on that jungle of a garden, and I see every leaf. And then, only then, does the horrible thought worm into my head that my father, God rest him, was right, and I shouldn't have chased Teddy. I shouldn't have made it happen. I shouldn't have led him like a lamb to the slaughter.

Then I look at Teddy reading in the browner-than-dirt armchair, and I feel my heart breaking. I hear it crackle inside me like burning sticks. The sound is so loud that the little flat trembles. He must hear it too. He must! The sound of my agonised heart must surely cut through his pages? But no. Nothing. He is absorbed.

"Teddy," I say in my sweetest and gentlest voice. "There must be more to living than this?"

He looks up, surprised. He weighs the question for a moment. "There isn't," he says. He returns to his book.

"Teddy," I say, sitting on the arm of his chair. "I want to try new things."

"I already have," he replies, patting my arm. "And they're not worth it. Take my word."

He strokes my cheek, turns a page, and the day trundles on, the crackle of my heart soon forgotten.

When it strikes me, the solution is clear as glass, staring me in the face like the goggly eyes of a fish. Tweedledum and Tweedledee, Barney and Beany, Bill and Ben. The answer to my doubts in a pram if not a nutshell. That is, when he is sober and I am sober, I am going to conceive a child. My own little baby in Teddy's arms, all gummy smiles and dribble. Her gorgeous wee clothes in the wardrobe, a rubber ducky in the bath and alphabet magnets on the fridge. So. Out with the pills and bits of rubber. In with the temperature charts and calculations.

Life becomes so simple when clearly divisible into fertile and non-fertile days.

On the former I skitter about the flat in my skin. I toss his book away and slither onto his lap. I arch my back like a cat. God, I am so sexy. Baby, baby, I think, pulling him into me. I soak him up like a sponge. I don't waste a drop. I can make it happen, watch me. The gurgling, kicking infant, her wee heart set going by love, the happily ever after. I can do it all.

"Jane," he says, "for years my desire to look after another living creature has been fulfilled by watering a rubber plant."

"Ssh," I say, tickling him again. We do it sideways, backwards, upside-down, leaving no part of my insides undrenched by his fluids.

Inevitably I get it right. I am testing positive, teeming, great with child. My breasts swell with my abdomen. Liquid oozes from my nipples. I am fruitful and exuberant. Pinker than candy floss. I wear pink, talk pink, think pink. I float in a glass bubble.

In the mornings Teddy and I sit side by side in the brown armchairs, lost in our books. My hand rests always on my bump, ready to monitor each flutter, inside and out. My book is from the library. It's called *Pregnancy*. I study the gorgeous pictures of developing foetuses. Twenty weeks. Twenty-four weeks. Twenty-eight weeks. "Look, Teddy, this one! This is what she looks like now."

Teddy glances at the page. "I can't be keen on a stranger that I've never met," he says.

I am not listening. I pour him out a whisky. I sing a lullaby, rocking an imaginary cradle with my toe. I glow.

Jesus, Mary and Joseph, she won't stop bawling! Great gasping howls that give me the shakes. Tiny flailing fists, red face! What'll I do? Oh my God, the baby's just puked down my front. Poor little mite. I'm frightened. If only she could tell me what's wrong with her. She is so helpless. Up and down the flat I march with her. Down and up. Anything to stop that ghastly wailing.

If only Teddy would come home.

God, I'm scared, scared to death. What if I drop her? No. I am not going to drop her. I wouldn't drop Gina. Not my darling baby girl. My darling. Baby. Howling girl. Poor thing. My God, I never realised how dark the night was.

She's gone quiet. At last. Sleeping, thank God. At least I think she's sleeping. I wonder. Is her neck right? It's like a stick. It could be twisted away like the stem of a cherry, that neck. "Calm down, Jane," I say out loud. My voice seems a ghost's. Of course she's asleep. I feel her little chest rising and falling. Peace. I mop at my pukey front with my free hand. Dear God, is that shit under my nail from her last nappy? I look in the mirror. Is that haggard bat in there really me? I pour myself out a whisky. I sit, looking at Gina's wee head as I drink. My heart is still thumping. I wonder just what the hell I'm doing, playing Mummy. Amn't I only a kid myself?

I listen to Teddy's jaunty footsteps on the stairs. His key turns in the lock. His happy hum fills the air. If he had a cane, he could dance as well as sing. He strides in, looking so like himself that I'm green. Not a hair on his shampooed head is out of place, especially round his eyebrows, which he does dye. I know he does because I found the bottle in his drawer underneath his boxer shorts.

"Get me another drink," I say.

"What's the smell?" he asks, pouring for us both.

"Puke," I say. I down the whisky in a gulp. "We've got to bring her to the pub tomorrow night. I can't be alone with her every night, sure I can't. You'll carry her, won't you, Teddy? I'll buy you a sling."

"You carry her," Teddy says. "It was your idea to have her."

"You did your bit. You." I plonk Gina into his arms. She opens her wee eyes, which focus upon his. Her lips quiver, then stretch. She is smiling at him, for God's sake! She looks gorgeous. "Oh, Teddy," I say melting, absolutely melting. "She adores you. You know I think this is the way it's meant to be."

He pats Gina's fuzzy head. He jiggles her onto his hip, fishing a cigarette out of his pocket. He lights up, puffing out a cloud of smoke. She watches him with big eyes.

It's one of those black, black mornings, when light streams in the window and I see, too clearly, every leaf in that damned jungle of a garden, where I'm not allowed to step. And I don't want to see. There are times when blindness is a comfort. So. I've taken a bottle, one wee soldier, down from the shelf in the kitchenette. That shelf! Teddy's so-called cellar (every happy home should have one), only the screws holding it up are decidedly loose. Hah!

He's here, of course. The Meistersinger. Backside glued to his Mammy's armchair, brown as dirt, nose stuck deep inside an account of the Napoleonic wars, for God's sake, wars about which I am proud of my utter ignorance. You'd think he'd have said, "Good morning, Jane." That's all. Only common courtesy. Not too much to ask after six years of marriage and one child. Or is it?

"Good morning, Teddy," I say. Pointedly.

No reaction. Not so much as a tremor of the dyed eyebrows. You'd think he was a toad, sitting motionless on a log. Damn it, he's just turned a page, making me into a liar. What the hell, I'll drink to that. Jane, the liar! Bottoms up!

I stalk round the chair. Once, twice. He doesn't look up. He is like an exhibit in a museum. Could those be dustballs that I see about his feet? I might get a feather and poke it under his nose to check if he's still breathing.

"Hey, you!" I shout. "Is anybody home?"

I fill my glass again, up to the brim. "Lover boy," I say. "What with Gina at school, and me with the day off from the effing boutique, a unique opportunity has presented itself for fornication. By which I mean coitus without interruptus. Why don't I dump a tub of yoghurt all over your whatsit and lick it off? Whaddya say, huh?"

Nothing. He says nothing.

"Have it your way then, Teddy," I mutter. "Only we're going to have to talk sometime, if only about money."

I open the window and drop the empty bottle into the forbidden garden. I bet there are snakes out in that garden. I'd like to make friends with those snakes. When I think of all the things that I used to worry about. Growing old, for example. And infidelity. There's heaps worse, I can see that now. What the hell, I wish there *was* another woman. Or even another man, ducky! Anything to shake us up and get the old circulation on the trot again. Anything except this perpetual nothingness, this treating me like I'm not here at all.

I open another bottle. I know what. I'll get a felt tipped pen and write all over him, I love you, I love you, I love you . . .

I walk over. I sit on the arm of his chair. "Teddy," I whisper. I trace my finger round the perfect whorls of his ear. "Love?" I say. "Tell me that I'm only dreaming."

But he reads on and on about the Napoleonic wars.

When Gina was a baby, he carried her in a sling, cosy against the velvet of his jacket. The day that we married, he swept me up the stairs in his arms.

"Love?" I say. "You can talk to me about the Napoleonic wars if that's what you want."

I pour myself out another drink. I might as well laugh since I can't cry. Perhaps I should pull the dyed eyebrows out of his head and sell them. There's a market for everything, or so they say.

"Teddy," I say, slapping his cheek. "You have to listen! Kids cost money. Soon a posse of nuns will be coming to collect Gina's school fees. What's more, your daughter would like a Barbie doll, seeing as everyone else in her class has one already. There's rent to be paid, and the phone, and that other account, the one so large that it gobbles up the rest. By which I mean to say that the lion's share of our money goes to buying you drink, Teddy!"

Thanks be to God. I have gained the man's attention at last. Finally, the toad with the eyebrows is stirring on its brown log. It is clearing the phlegm from its throat. Believe me, I am all ears.

"You drink as much as I do," he says.

What? I reel backwards, amazed, the whisky sloshing in the blue bowl of my glass. "Are you joking?" I snarl. "Me? Jane? I hardly drink a drop. Only the occasional short, down the hatch to cheer me up, and God knows I need cheering with the life that I lead. No way do I drink too much. Besides, I hold it like a sailor."

I empty the shelf. I root them out from every corner and cupboard. I line them up on the table. The glass glitters, casting lozenges of colour onto the pale wall. So many bottles, rows of soldiers. Jewels of fire. One by one, I pour them down the drain, left-right, left-right. Only one remains. Lone soldier. My hand freezes on its neck. My mouth is a desert of sawdust and old cheese. "Dry!" I finally cry, spraying the bottle's contents into the sink. The word bangs inside my head. Sweat drizzles down my temple. My body burns for the lost drink. Teeth rattle in their sockets. Every bone cries out its need. Fire water, healer of woes! Let me lick it out of the sink!

I don't. I won't!

Insides kinked, I curl up on a foul armchair, blanketed with maggots. A pitiful specimen of humanity, queen of the rats, flesh and muck, remnant of a woman.

"You can't be serious," he says. Teddy sways slightly, a sheepish grin on his face.

"No more bottles," I repeat. I am hardly able to stand.

His lip curls. "You'll never stick it. You haven't the guts."

"If you bring so much as one bottle into this flat, I'll smash it," I roar. Trembling, I take his hand. "Help me, Teddy," I beg. "Come with me. Together is better than alone."

"You used to be such fun," he murmurs, shaking his head. "I have been a boozer for years. I am too old to change now."

Whistling cheerfully, Teddy bumps the door closed with his backside. He's lugging two enormous glass jugs, tins of concentrate, yeast, corks. "I am going to make my own," he says. "I am going to economise. Your bills will be paid and Gina can have her Barbie doll after all." He begins to kiss me purposefully, breathing his boozy breath into my mouth. His mouth tastes good, his body feels good, his warm, warm body at last curling again into my own. My God, he hasn't kissed me like this for years. He pulls away suddenly. "If you smash these jugs," he says, "I'll kill you."

He sets up the apparatus under the bed. "Ba-lop, ba-lop." The noise pursues me all around the flat. "Ba-lop, ba-lop." At night, as I lie open-eyed in his mother's bed, I can smell the wine fermenting beneath us. My throat is studded with pins.

"You'll never stick it," he whispers. "You haven't the guts."

Relics. It's all there waiting for Teddy, formally arranged on the table, the insides of my Teddy box exposed to the white light. What I was never going to show him for fear that he'd laugh. But I won't hear his footsteps coming up the stairs. I won't see his face when he picks up the little bread van, that precious dinky, held once in his little boy hands. Such love, such terrible aching love. Oh, Teddy, if only we could have stayed children together forever!

I look at my watch. Forty-five minutes to closing time. Forty-five minutes of a marriage left. The tap dry, the plug-hole open, the slops swirling down the drain. God, what a night. This is alone.

Gina's buggy is waiting. And a single bag. Most of our things are already gone. I've carted them out, bit by bit, right in front of his nose. He didn't even notice. Dear God.

I close my eyes. I hear it in my head. The echoing notes of the piano. The piano that my mother played in the hollow house of my childhood. That shocking house that I'm only beginning to understand now. I hear it in my head, the Faust waltz, tinkling, forever tinkling, played eternally by my mother's slender fingers. It fills me with shame, that waltz. I imagined my mother the enemy. She was no enemy, no, only an unfortunate woman, eaten away by life until she was a shell. I thought that I knew it all, then. I really did. At least I can still laugh. I hope she's up in heaven now, my mother, laughing her heart out with me, poor fool that I am, and at the mess that I've made of my life.

I lift my sleeping child into the buggy. Outside the night is magnificent. Am I stepping at last into the forbidden garden? "The stars are lighting the way for us, darling," I whisper. "God bless us, Gina."

It's all in my hands now. Only I'm not laughing anymore. I think I'm crying. My cheeks are wet. Jane, the child who never cried, is shuddering in the night, racked by great tears. Tears for myself, for all the precious hours that I've thrown away. Yes, I am crying. Crying because I am halfway through my life, and I'm just beginning to live.

The Naughty Bits

As the children play at my feet, I float from space to space.

I see it clearly, each outline etched against a white light. The coffin is closed. The air smells familiar, that dry faint smell of smoke which clings to the things that she sends me. They are stacked around the coffin, these things, envelopes bulging with newspaper cuttings. White and grey envelopes in towering stacks. Large manila ones with her own name thriftily scratched out and readdressed to me.

She is not dead. But the possibility of death shades every day. The distance I have created between us is no buffer. Each ring of the telephone threatens. I tremble as I raise the receiver. Is this it? I have dreamed a thousand times. Is this the end?

I am writing a novel about a woman, a young woman who ran away. As I write, the children play at my feet. The girl is sunny and blonde. She chatters happily with strangers and jumps into the arms of friends. The boy is more cautious. He never seems to listen, but he misses nothing. I imagine that he might be like I was. They play computers, these children. They have rearranged our living space and recreated each object as a machine. The table, the chair, the lamp with the Chinese shade, the sofa: all are part of their fun. The real computer sits silent in a corner. These children recognise no limits.

I remember being a child. The beds are pushed into the middle of the room. She is making them angrily. Her slippers slap hard against the carpet as she moves. I play dolls at her feet. She reaches out to smack me, hard. I see her great hand rising in the air, hesitating as it gains strength, then flying sharply down. I watch, and at the last moment, scuttle sideways to safety. She brings her hand down hard upon her own thigh. A red weal erupts angrily on her skin. I learn to play at a safer distance.

I would like to say that I do not strike my own children, but it would not be true. I do not hit them often, but when I do, a choking feeling comes upon me. I feel her hand upon me, her flesh upon my flesh. I sense myself sliding out from her body, as my children have emerged from mine.

The children jump and laugh. They have transformed our house into a circus of light and energy. The computer chair sings. "Buzzy-bee! Buzzy-bee!" chants the girl. "Buzzy-bee! The table computer's all yellow and black! Buzzy-bee!"

"Yes! YES! *YES!!*" raves the boy. "I got him! The alien

140

from Mars! He's dead meat!" The boy flings himself onto the sofa in delight. The girl leaps on top, wild with joy.

I write about rebellion. As they wrestle and laugh, I write steadily of rebellion. I have written about other things, the strange flotsam of life, the butchers, the bakers, the candlestick makers. But after each subject has worked itself through my head, my words cycle back relentlessly to rebellion. It is my lasting obsession.

I hear the envelope drop through the letterbox. "Post," yells the boy. Together, they thunder to the door. The girl is first, but she cannot read. Impatiently, he peers over her shoulder, longing to snatch, but knowing it's not allowed. "It's for you, Mummy," he calls. I weigh the envelope in my hands. It is too fat to contain what I really want. Still I search through the newspaper cuttings hopefully. The whiff of her cigarettes burns my nostrils, but there is no letter. Disappointed, I let the cuttings flutter to the floor, bits of paper touched by her fingers. I picture her there in the high-ceilinged room, rooted stiffly to her towering chair, cutting, cutting obsessively. I see the scissors attached by a chain to her waist. I am certain that she thinks of me as relentlessly as I think of her. But just what does she think? Why does she fall back on the words that she reads, rather than those she thinks, to communicate?

I pick up my pen and I write of rebellion. The children trumpet about me. I fill page after page with my distinctive clear script, neatly shaped words that any child could read. Her writing is like a maze, elegant and illegible.

I leave my rebellious pages on the floor with the

children's games and stretch for the album on the top
shelf. It is the one with Marilyn Monroe on its cover, her
white skirt billowing. Inside are the bits and pieces of my
teenage self, carefully preserved under plastic. I study the
photographs wryly. My young face heavy with make-up.
Skirts hitched up at the waist to bare my thighs. White
ankle boots with black fish-net tights.

There's a print, too. St George and the dragon, with
three fiery heads, each with her features crudely pencilled
in by my angry hand. I see myself skipping home to her,
heart fluttering with girlish excitement. I need to share
my triumph, the heavy bracelet jangling on my arm, the
promise of some youth's undying love. I expect her to toss
her head happily, to bask in my success. But she stares at
me like a fish. "Take it back at once!" she screams, her
face twisting into nastiness. "Lolita! Don't let me catch
you near him again!" I don't. Let her catch me. I learn to
conceal that bodily part of myself from her, and
everything else as well.

I take my teenage revenge. I invent a mistress for my
father, a blonde woman with one blue eye and one brown
eye. She wears a velvet coat that brushes her ankles, and
she is named Natasha. She is one in a million, and she
adores me. She gushes over the bracelet, and weighs
seriously the question of flowers at my distant wedding.
Lilies of the valley or roses? She is there to confide in, my
father's mistress, on that first magic occasion when a
youth's fingers drift casually across my breast. With the
encouragement of my father's mistress, I open out like a
flower.

At my feet, the children play. The boy knocks against me, arrogance in his little body. "I'm going to give that computer table a kick up the arse." His eye glints with the knowledge of his own naughtiness. I stare him down. "I'm going to give that table computer . . ." He begins less firmly, then hesitates. "A kick up the Arsenal!" He rocks with laughter, delighted with his own invention. "That's OK, Mummy, isn't it? Arsenal? It's a football team."

I am older now. So is she. Her face is lined and her voice softened. She is not the villainess that she was. I see her infrequently; it is the distance I have created between us; she is always with me. I have taken to sending her what I write. I write about rebellion; it is my only theme. I am nearing forty, and what do I care for her approval?

I don't do things her way. She despises mine. But what does it matter? It might be easy to wrong your children. Did I ever ask what it was in her life that drove her? Was there something dark and bitter, something that she could not fathom? Why does she sit there now, rooted in the high-backed chair, with scissors attached by a chain to her waist, cutting, cutting, cutting?

It is possible that I send her my writing – shaped formal words – just in the way that she sends me newsprint. It might be the same, invented verbiage to throw up dust upon what we feel for each other.

I dream. I dream that the phone rings and for once I do not tremble as I raise the receiver. I know it is her, my mother, alive and jubilant. She has read my novel, my novel about the young woman who ran away. "I like the

naughty bits," she says firmly. "I *love* your naughty bits!"
She shouts it to the skies and her voice flies over the
space between us. It is strong and young, and our whole
life trembles before us.

The envelope thuds through the letterbox. My
children rush to get it. I tear it open with my teeth and
cuttings flutter to the floor. There is no letter.

"Mummy, Mummy!" My eyes blink open. The boy
stands before me, his face white with fear. The girl
cowers behind him, clutching the Chinese lampshade to
her breast. Great, white shards of pottery are sprayed
across the carpet, pinning my manuscript to the floor.
The lamp with the Chinese shade, gone forever.

Fury surges inside me. I raise my arm to strike them.
The girl bursts into tears. Something holds back my
hand. A voice hammers inside my head. "I like your
naughty bits."

The boy's arm creeps round the waist of his sobbing
sister. Shivering and helpless, they await my judgment.
Their eyes are pools which reflect the terribleness of the
deed that they have committed. It is punishment
enough. "I like your naughty bits." It is my own voice
that I hear. I am with my children in our living-room.
They are my children and I love them.

"I'm sorry," the boy says, scared. "Aren't you going to
smack us?"

I regret the loss of my lamp. But I didn't stop them
playing with it. It is not their fault alone. "We had all
better save our pennies for a new one." The mildness in
my voice soothes our stretched nerves.

"Daddy, too?" the boy chimes hopefully. Lightly we pick up the pieces together and take them out to the kitchen. I am so lucky. I am luckier than she was.

Perhaps she'll never say what I want her to say. But the answer lies within me. The cycle can be broken. I will ring her up. I will tell her that I love her, even though . . . I will tell her that I love her, if she . . . I will tell her that I love her.